385

Katherine
Robertson

Manufactured in Canada by Webcom.

Cover painting by Gustavo Novoa.
Cover lay-out by Art Gardner.

ISBN 0-919951-10-4

THE COVER

The painting on the cover of this book was done by the talented New York artist, Gustavo Novoa, who also happens to be my kind friend. Thank you, Gustavo, for capturing so beautifully the enchantment of...

The Scarlet Castle

ACKNOWLEDGEMENT

In ages past, writers often credited "the Muse" with whatever of creative merit their works might have embodied. While such kindly but incorporeal counsellors could well exist, I myself am fortunate to have had a more directly accessible advisor to help me with the writing of *The Scarlet Castle*. This friend, whom I shall simply call "H", has been an inexhaustible source of guidance and inspiration throughout the preparation of this text, and I wish here to express my deep appreciation for all he has done to make this book a reality.

Maurice B. Cooke.

DEDICATION

This book is lovingly dedicated
to my four beautiful children:
Tiffany, Noel, Charles and Samantha.

THE SCARLET CASTLE
A Tale of Fantasy for All Ages

First Book of Moralia
Maurice B.Cooke

ONE

Moralia is a distant land far beyond the last colour of the last rainbow, a mystical place that adults never speak of but all the children remember, where the light comes in from everywhere and summer goes on forever. It is a country where wishes come true instantly, and tall people do not always decide what you must do and where you must go.

If you wish to be alone and quiet by yourself, you can find vast forest glades where not the shimmer of a sound disturbs the reigning silence, nor the rustle of a vagrant leaf invades the reverie of calm.

Yet should you prefer the wonder of great buildings and the bustle of crowds, there are giant cities of crystal glass and soaring spires, with mighty temples where the holy breath comes forth from the air itself, and wondrous pyramids where the power of creation hums in the heart of every stone.

Many folk would not believe that such a place could possibly exist, because their minds dwell only on the dreary episodes of their everyday lives, or the dull grey sadness of lost enthusiasms, or the tedious round of working and sleeping that has caught them in its coils. They do not see that these dismal monotonies are but wraiths — insubstantial shadows that their minds have cast up before them — and that, like all shadows, they can be banished in an instant by the brightness of a happy thought, the illumination of a gladdened heart, or the unquenchable light in the eyes of one who truly loves.

But let us return to Moralia. Once long ago in this beautiful land there lived a gentle sprite called Tenuli, a sweet and innocent little being with wide eyes, slender arms and legs, and a purity of heart that one could never find in this world.

Tenuli spent most of her time sitting by the Great River that ran through Moralia, listening to its deep continual voice unravelling the mysteries of life for all who could hear from within. Many of the lessons she understood, yet there was much that Tenuli could not grasp for it went beyond her own experience. Whenever her puzzlement became too great, she would go to the giant Temple of Learning and ask one of the teachers to help her understand. Her favorite was Jelander, for he always smiled so kindly whenever he saw her approach, and his gentle voice seemed to come more from his heart than from his throat.

Tenuli had also another dear friend, whom she especially loved. This was Doran, an older sprite who had seen much of the worlds beyond Moralia, and who had even gone down several times into the Shadowland, to help restore light among the inhabitants of that darkened world.

One day Tenuli was sitting with Doran on the banks of the Great River, talking of many things. Occasionally they would fall silent, listening to the voice of the waters. It was during one of these silent intervals that she first heard the river speak of pain, and of how quickly pain could teach the lessons of life. Never before had she heard about pain, and she immediately asked Doran what it meant.

"Tenuli, you have never felt the thing called pain," he said slowly. "I fear I shall not be able to find anything in your life with which to compare it."

"But surely *you* have felt this... pain?"

Doran stared cloudily into the deep river and did not answer at first. Then he said, "in the Shadowland there is much pain, but not here. You have never been to that place, and therefore you cannot know what it is like."

"But Doran, *try* to explain it to me," she implored, her wide eyes looking up at him with an expression of perfect trust.

"Little Tenuli," he smiled, "how innocent you are. Very well, I shall try my best. Do you know how sometimes you find only confusion in the words of the river, and the confusion impels you at last to seek out Jelander or one of the other teachers?"

"Yes of course."

"Well, the confusion is like a prod that pushes you to do something — like going to the Temple of Learning. In the same way, the experience of pain in the Shadowland

2

prompts the inhabitants of that world to do something to stop the pain. That something is often to change a habit or learn a truth which otherwise they would not change or learn."

"So pain is like when I do not understand the Great River?"

"Not exactly, but just like your puzzlement it is a spur to action. In the Shadowland one does not wish to continue feeling pain, hence it is an encouragement to do something to stop it."

"But Doran, what makes the pain in the Shadowland?"

"Many things, Tenuli," he replied, "but most pain comes from not having learned to approach life there in the right way. Many in the Shadowland become greatly attached to things or circumstances in that world, and then when the things are lost or the circumstances change, they are very unhappy. This unhappiness is one form of pain."

"But why would anyone become attached in that way? Are not all things free? Does not the Great Light care for them all?"

"Of course, but most of the inhabitants of the Shadowland do not see that. They think they must rely only upon themselves for everything, and have forgotten that the Great Light embraces them all and is in them all. This thought has cast a layer of darkness upon their little world, and through this darkness the Great Light cannot easily shine."

"All pain is because they do not understand?"

"No. Some pain comes as an illness of the body, because of their thoughts or feelings. When they fill long years with resentment or fear or worry—"

"Those are words I do not know, Doran," she interrupted. "What do they mean?"

Again Doran fell silent. After a moment he turned to Tenuli and said, "sweet innocent sprite, perhaps it is time for you to find out these things for yourself. You have learned much from the Great River, but there is more that can be learned only in the Shadowland. If you wish, we can find Jelander and talk about it with him."

Tenuli felt a thrill of anticipation. She knew that almost all sprites eventually reach the stage where they enter the Shadowland for periods of time. And she remembered that whenever Doran had returned to Moralia from that place there was always something different about him — a new light in his eyes, a deeper capacity to understand things, a broader love in his heart.

And she knew in the instant Doran suggested it that now was her time to go.

TWO

The temple of Learning loomed before them as Tenuli and Doran walked in silence along the treed path which led to that great structure. From a time before the misty beginnings of Moralia itself, this beautiful building had been the guardian of all that the Moralians had ever known or understood about their world. Four crystal spires rose high at the corners of a central pyramid of immense size. It was flanked on three sides with pure gold and on the fourth with iron, signifying the idea that each being contained the three golden principles of mind, heart and will... and a fourth factor — an unknown nebulous shading that could be strengthened like iron when it becomes steel, or could be weakened like iron when it rusts. This was to remind all who studied at the temple that there was a task set for each individual, a challenge to take up the raw material of his own being, refining and molding it until, shaped at last to its purest and strongest form, it could reflect back undistorted the Great Light that cascaded from everywhere to everywhere.

Yet the challenge also carried with it a danger: that without vigilant care, the nebulous shading could darken down to a deeper and deeper hue, until finally it became a weight of blackness that would obscure even the Great Light from view.

Tenuli and Doran had walked together many times to the Temple of Learning, but never had she felt such anticipation, as if all the previous steps on her path had been but

4

a preparation for this new adventure. She remembered that the Great River had spoken often of the purpose served by the Shadowland, explaining that a sojourn in that lower world helped to quicken one's discernment and expand one's wisdom. By seeking to remain true to one's highest goals, even when faced with the shades of imagined things that obscured the light from view, one could learn persistence, courage, honour ...

But little Tenuli had not understood all of these ideas that rode the voice of the waters. What was persistence? What was courage? She sensed now, as they mounted the wide alabaster steps to the central pyramid, that at last she would learn these things, at last she would understand in the same deep way that Doran did. And she yearned to be more like him, knowing that it would help to broaden her love for her dear friend.

They found Jelander by the sparkling fountain that fell in a billion rainbow droplets down the very center of the pyramid. He was talking with two young sprites about one of the higher worlds, explaining that Moralia was a place of preparation for the loftier levels, just as the Shadowland helped to improve and strengthen the Moralians who went down there to live for a time.

"Goldenland," he was saying, "ah yes, I have seen it with my own eyes. But it is not yet time for me to go there permanently. I must remain here as a teacher yet a while, for it is part of my path to help others understand. Until my debt is discharged I cannot be free of Moralia." Then he caught sight of Tenuli and Doran as they approached. "Hah!" he exclaimed with a broad grin, "my little Tuli comes with her friend. And how has His Gracious Wetness confused you today, little sprite?"

She placed both of her hands in his, and could feel the kindly love in his touch. "Jelander," she began, "you have helped me to understand many things. But I fear that even you cannot teach me to know pain, or the changes it brings. I yearn to understand more of life. What must I do to gain entrance to the Shadowland?"

"Ah, so you have heard this idea from the Great River,"

5

he began slowly. "And what says Doran to this plan of yours?"

She answered, "it was he who explained that pain is known only in the lower world. But Jelander, when I heard his words, I knew in my heart that it was my time to visit that land. Can you give me your counsel?"

"Let us sit in the orchard behind the Temple," replied Jelander. "We shall talk of this matter further." He bid farewell to the other sprites with whom he had been speaking, and led the way through the arch that opened on the orchard.

The trees were in full bloom, stretching away from the portal in a breathtaking panorama of colour and scent. Tiny songbirds floated their notes of joy upon the sweet air, while butterflies chased each other along spasmodic paths through the blossoming branches. Here and there under the trees were wooden benches, set in groupings to allow several people to sit comfortably in conversation.

When they were settled, Jelander leaned forward and took Tenuli's right hand between both of his. "Tuli," he began, "I knew that you would seek me out on this matter. The Great River always teaches his truth in cycles, with each thought building upon the one before. I too pay heed to the voice of the waters, and I understood that it would soon speak of the gift of pain. If you feel from within that it is time for you to enter the Shadowland, then we shall arrange it. But first you must know all that the experience requires. Here in Moralia it is easy to remember that you are sheltered and cared for by the Great Light that shines from everywhere to everywhere. But in the Shadowland you will gradually forget your life here, your friends—"

"Forget!" cried Tenuli. "Never! How could I not remember your kindness, or Doran's sweet face, or the many times I have sat by the Great River?"

"Nevertheless," said Jelander patiently, "you shall find it harder and harder to recall your life in Moralia. It is the nature of the Shadowland to obscure the memory in that way. Then there are the Laws of Entry. All Moralians who wish to sojourn in the Shadowland must agree to two conditions: first they must accept a mission, a special task which they are to perform while in the Shadowland; second they must enter the Shadowland along one of the Pathways of Change, for in so doing they arrive with certain new qualities, which lead to faster learning than can take place here."

"But I do not understand that, Jelander."

The old teacher sat back and looked over to Doran. "Perhaps your friend can explain it as well as I. He has passed many times along the Pathways of Change."

Doran thought a moment, then said, "yes, in my case the changes were beneficial in the end, though while I was in the Shadowland it was very hard."

"What do you mean?" asked Tenuli, now more confused than ever.

"You know me as quiet and reserved, I think. Is that not so?"

"Yes, you are slow to speak, Doran."

"Once when I was to begin a sojourn in Shadowland, it was decided that I had not ever learned what it was to use the tongue in a hurtful way. It was felt that my habit of saying little came more from simple shyness than from a desire to avoid offending or wounding others with my words. So the Sixth Pathway was chosen for me, knowing that those entering along this ray would be quick to voice criticism of others. I accepted that change, and when I arrived in the Shadowland, I began to be dissatisfied with the faults in those around me, forgetting that these faults were usually due to the Pathways of Change along which they had entered. I became intolerant and began to criticise my friends, thinking that I was helping them by pointing out their flaws. Alas! All I did was to drive a wedge in between us. And in the pain of my separation and loneliness, I came to understand the value of tolerance and forgiveness, the importance of remaining silent rather than giving offence with my words. Unless you have experienced the changes yourself, little friend, you cannot know. In my case, the criticism, the habit of passing judgement on the faults of others, was *itself* a major fault. But only

7

by going through that bitter experience of loneliness brought on by my own actions, could I have truly understood this great lesson."

"Is there a special… flaw for each Pathway then?"

Jelander answered her. "Twelve Pathways, twelve flaws," he said. "We shall consider what is the best Pathway for you after we have decided on your mission."

"I will do whatever you ask, kind Jelander."

"Be not hasty," the older man replied. "We have of course something in mind for you. But you are free to accept or reject it. Think carefully before replying."

Tenuli suddenly realized that both Jelander and Doran had known that she would soon reach the point of wanting an experience in the Shadowland, and that they already had planned and discussed the details of her first adventure in that place. She turned her wide eyes on Doran. "Well, my silent friend," she said, "you did not say all that you knew of these things."

"Forgive me, dear Tenuli, but we had to wait for you to show that you were ready for this adventure. It is the law."

Tenuli smiled her love at him.

Jelander began speaking. She listened fascinated as he explained the conditions in the lower world at that time. The Prince of Shades, he told her, had managed to establish a powerful position for himself there, and using dreadfully cruel methods had erected a stronghold which was called the Scarlet Castle. The slaves who had built the castle for him had been mercilessly flogged, and the blood from their whip wounds had dyed the stones of its wall a deep red. Yet years of rain and snow had not washed away the scarlet colour, and it remained a signal of evil that could be read by any who still understood the meaning of signs. But there were few such discerning people now in the Shadowland, and the cruelty of the castle's beginning had been conveniently forgotten.

The castle itself stood on an outcropping of barren rock six miles to the south of the Grey City, and was reached by a single roadway that climbed its gentler slope. It was rumoured that an underground passage had been chisled through the living rock to a hidden entrance opposite the main road, but none of the Shadowlanders knew precisely where that entrance was located.

Stretching east from the castle were the Plains of Mordan, a level region of sparse grasses and stunted bush, under whose dry, lifeless soil the slaves who had died building the castle had been buried in mass graves. Ever since the day when the last slave was laid to rest, not a breath of wind had stirred above the Plains of Mordan. It was said that the air itself had become lifeless in sympathy for those who had been flogged to death against the stones they were working. And it was believed that, if ever a day came when the air began to blow again over the Plains of Mordan, on that same day the Scarlet Castle would be destroyed forever.

The Prince of Shades had managed to entice many of the inhabitants of Shadowland into living with him in the castle, by appealing to their baser instincts. One of these was Eluron, whom Tenuli had known when he had last been in Moralia. She remembered Eluron's quiet, sad eyes and slow way of walking, and she realized that she had not seen him for a long time.

Eluron had last entered the Shadowland along the second pathway of change, which causes a tendency to overvalue material things in general, and money in particular. Tenuli did not understand what money was, since it was not needed in Moralia, but Jelander explained that its use in the Shadowland had arisen through a mistrustful and selfish streak in the inhabitants of that world which had led to a habit of bartering among each other for various goods, and that eventually money had begun to circulate as a means to make the bartering easier. But now, he told her, the evil thorn of greed had sprung up everywhere and most Shadowlanders had succumbed to the temptation of hoarding to themselves as much as they could get of everything. The result was that a few powerful individuals had control of most of the wealth, while the majority had little they could call their own, nor any way of obtaining the

9

basic necessities.

"But I don't understand... necessities," said Tenuli.

"Here in Moralia everything is provided by the Great Light which shines from everywhere to everywhere," Jelander replied, "but it is not so in the Shadowland. In that place everyone fears scarcity, and their fears deepen even more the darkness of the lower world.

Tenuli listened spellbound as Jelander described what had happened to her friend, and the dreadful things that were then occurring in the Shadowland.

Eluron had gone to the lower world with the intention of learning not to overvalue money and possessions. In earlier sojourns in the Shadowland, he had repeatedly given in to that temptation, and had finally acquired a permanent habit of stinginess and possessiveness. This unfortunate trait was causing difficulties for him whenever he would return to Moralia. He found it harder and harder to understand the voice of the waters. He could no longer gaze directly at the Great Light and took to wearing a hood to shelter his eyes from the brightness. And many of his former friends had started to avoid him, for they found his long, morose silences hard to bear.

At length he had come for counsel to his old teacher at the Temple of Learning, whose name was Trillamar. After much discussion as to the cause of the sadness that had crept over Eluron, it was decided to send him back once more into the Shadowland — this time along the Second Pathway, so that his habit of materiality and possessiveness would be *magnified and increased.* According to the plan, this would cause him to embark on a course which would lead him finally to a momentous choice — the most crucial he had ever faced: either to side with evil and slip further down into the quagmire of avarice, or to shake himself free of his slavery to greed, and with one giant leap back into the light, plant his feet squarely on the upward path. To accomplish this, Eluron would have to undergo an adventure in which the qualities of action, courage and resourcefulness would be forced to surface within him — qualities that he did not ordinarily possess. These noble traits would restore to Eluron the feeling of self-respect and wholeness that he had somehow lost in previous sojourns in the Shadowland, for it was that loss which lay behind Eluron's avarice and greed: he had come to rely on possessions for his sense of worth.

Thus his personal goal of learning was to dismantle his unfortunate tendency to crave money and material things above all else.

But he was also required to carry out a mission in the Shadowland. That mission was to learn the whereabouts of the secret entrance to the Scarlet Castle and pass the information to the Knight of Roses, who was planning a campaign against the evil Prince of Shades. The Knight led a small band of dedicated followers who had managed to retain a dim memory of the love and beauty in Moralia (from which, of course, they all had come). Because of that memory, these individuals could not be tricked into thinking that the Shadowland was all there was to reality, nor that the darkness of that sad place was the only condition under which people could live. They longed to banish the shadows so that the Great Light could illuminate the lower world just as it did the higher one. But they knew that so long as the Prince of Shades remained secure in the Scarlet Castle, and so long as there were people in the Shadowland who gave him their allegiance, the Great Light would never be seen.

Eluron had accepted the goal and the mission, desperate to be done with the melancholy that had gripped his being. Trillamar had arranged to project him into the Shadowland at a town not far from the Grey City, called Sandria. Now Sandria was really nothing more than a huddle of simple dwellings clustered around a central square, but that square contained something which had caused the name of Sandria to become known throughout the land of shadows. This was the famous Well of Tears, an ancient stone watering place whose beginnings were lost in antiquity. The legend of Sandria said that once, thousands of years before, the dark layer of dense cloud that hovered impenetrably over the land of shadows had been broken;

that for one shining hour a great golden orb of light had been revealed in the sky; and that a brilliant ray from that searing eye had fallen on the place that was now Sandria. When at last the clouds closed over to bring again the grey half-light of Shadowland, the Well of Tears had miraculously appeared.

The well itself had the familiar form of all wells: a circular wall of stone surrounding a deep hole in the ground. The water level in the well was about twelve feet below the top, and the water itself was of a crystal purity found nowhere else in the land of shadows.

It was said that when you looked down into the well at your own reflection, a memory would come to you — the memory of a wondrous land of light and joy — and that if you drank from the well you would understand for a brief instant why you had abandoned that illuminated place to sojourn in the land of shadows. It was a realization that flickered and then was gone — a fleeting glimpse of truth soon replaced by the heavier thoughts of everyday life. Always the experience brought tears of joy, of recognition, to the eyes. And that is how the well was named.

From the far corners of Shadowland pilgrims would come to Sandria, for despite the grey dimness which engulfed everything in that land, there were yet a few people who yearned for something beyond the drab monotonies of the lower world. Although they had forgotten the details of Moralia, still somewhere in the back of their minds they remembered a certain feeling, a flicker of hope and joy, a dim sense of lightness and freedom and love that were not to be found in the land of shadows.

And of course the followers of the Knight of Roses regularly made pilgrimage to the Well of Tears, so that their memory of a higher light could be rekindled, and their determination to oust the Prince of Shades could harden.

Jelander rose from the bench and helped Tenuli to her feet. "Now I must show you exactly what happened to Eluron just after he entered the lower world," he said. "It will help you to understand better your own mission there. We will go to the Apex Room in the Temple of

12

Learning and look into the Crystal of Remembrance."

Doran and Tenuli followed Jelander back into the pyramid, and up to a small room under the peak of the building. In the center of the room, mounted on inverted claws of fine gold, were three spheres of crystal set in a triangle. They were about one foot in diameter, and identical in all respects except for colour. One of them had a blue tint, a second appeared faintly reddish, and the third was clear.

Jelander pointed to the reddish sphere. "The Crystal of Remembrance," he said. "It allows us to review that which has already taken place in the Shadowland. The blue one is the Crystal of Projection, which gives us pictures of the most probable future events in the lower world. That other is the Crystal of Forever. Through it we can watch the things happening right now in the land of shadows."

"How do they work?" Tenuli asked.

"The crystals respond only to mental commands," smiled Jelander. "We must be trained to operate them. Watch the red one now. I will focus it back to Eluron's appearance in the Shadowland, right next to the Well of Tears."

The little room seemed to darken as the Crystal of Remembrance began to glow from within. Misty images formed themselves on its surface as Tenuli watched fascinated. Then the picture cleared and she saw a figure lying on the ground — a figure she recognized as Eluron. They looked on as the scene unfolded...

*　*　*

Eluron rose unsteadily to his feet, trying to gather his thoughts together. He looked around him, and caught sight of the Well of Tears only a short distance away. Taking a few steps, he quickly found his balance, then walked over to the well.

Halting just short of the round stone wall, Eluron gingerly reached out his hand... then hesitated, suddenly suspecting that merely by touching the wall something unexpected would occur.

His fingers contacted the cold, wet stone. Immediately a vibration ran through his body like a mild electrical shock. Swiftly he pulled back his hand, shaking it to get rid of the odd sensation.

All during these initial moments in the Shadowland, Eluron's mind had been struggling to retain a remembrance of the place he had just left behind. Dimly he recalled the name Moralia, and even more dimly swam the face of Trillamar in his memory. The amnesia which the Shadowland forces upon all who visit that world was gradually strengthening its grip on his mind.

But it had been deliberately planned to project him into the lower dimension close to the Well of Tears, with the expectation that his curiosity would impell him to approach the well, look down into its limpid clarity, and drink the water. This experience, it was hoped, would briefly illuminate in his mind the purpose for which he had come, and in addition would acquaint him with a location to which he could return whenever he wanted to recall his true purpose in the Shadowland.

Now he stood uncertainly, not sure that he wanted again to experience the odd vibrations that came upon touching the stone wall. Then he made up his mind, turned on his heel, and strode off toward the Grey City — whose dreary outline he could perceive in the distance.

THREE

As Eluron advanced toward the edge of the city, he tried to keep in his mind the light and pleasant picture of Moralia — its bright colourful landscapes, the gentle faces of its inhabitants — but slowly the memory faded, until by the time he had reached the outskirts, he could remember nothing beyond his own name.

"He's a big one, ain't he?" came a rough voice as Eluron passed the darkened doorway of what appeared to be an abandoned building at the edge of the city.

"An' he looks new to these parts, too," answered another, thinner voice. This was followed by a coughing fit and a few muttered cursewords.

"Your name, my man," said the first voice, and this time Eluron could see the dim outline of a huge figure in the doorway, evidently the owner of the voice, as it took a step closer to him.

"Eluron," he replied, not sure whether to stay or run.

"A fancy name, that one," said the other voice. "Let's have a look at 'im."

Out of the doorway walked a giant of a man, standing a full head taller than Eluron, and with him came a crippled companion who barely rose to the giant's elbow.

"Let's see if he's got any money," said the cripple.

The giant had stopped and was looking intently at Eluron. "Be still, Milo," he replied, "I think I know this one."

Eluron looked back into the giant's face and he too felt a flash of recognition, but the details of where or how he might once have known the large man hovered just beyond his reach.

"Are you one of the Stalkers, like us?" asked the giant.

"I think I have just arrived in this place," said Eluron uncertainly.

"Humph," grunted the other, "maybe I don't recognize you after all. Still, you seem a bully sort. Come along, we'll take you to Korak. Maybe he will want you to be one of us."

Eluron was confused by this sudden turn of events. He had expected to be accosted and perhaps beaten by these two, and yet the large man appeared to be offering some sort of gruff friendship. Having no other immediate plans, Eluron decided to accompany them and at least talk to this Korak person, whoever he was. "Lead on," he said.

They set off along an alleyway past a number of structures that looked like abandoned warehouses, and at length came to a trap-door that opened to reveal a set of stairs leading down along a subterranean passageway. Tallow candles flickered at intervals as they moved single-file down the steps, causing fitful shadows to leap and dance against the dark stone walls...

15

* * *

Now the picture in the red crystal became frozen like a snapshot, as the door to the Apex Room opened to admit Trillamar, Eluron's teacher. He greeted the others, then looked at the picture in the Crystal of Remembrance and smiled. Seating himself, he began to describe who the other two men were.

The giant figure leading the way was Hindalom, he said, a very forceful individual who had volunteered to enter the Shadowland along the First Pathway of Change — that which gives one a great deal of physical strength. Trillamar explained that in previous sojourns in the lower world, Hindalom had repeatedly fallen in with the criminal element and had adopted a habit of using brute strength to take what he wanted from those who were weaker. By sending him down along the First Pathway, that forceful nature would be enhanced; but it had been planned that, if Hindalom again yielded to the same temptation, a serious physical illness would seize his body and render him as weak as a kitten. Through that experience, it was hoped that he would learn not to use his strength to bring distress or pain to others.

Milo too had been an individual who during stays in the Shadowland had taken to using force in order to impel others to do his will. In his case it had been decided to send him down along a particular part of the Fourth Pathway which would result in an inherent weakness of the body. Then, an accident would be arranged which, due to the inherent weakness, would result in a permanent crippling. By being thus deprived of the strength necessary to bully others, it was expected that Milo would unlearn this wrongful habit. Hindalom and Milo were actually good friends when in Moralia, and it was part of the plan to have the larger man befriend and take care of Milo, so that the latter could be on the receiving end of kindness, albeit of a rough-and-ready sort. This demonstration of friendship, it was hoped, would teach Milo that even the worst of scoundrels had some redeeming feature, thus encoura-

16

ging him to fan the embers of his own goodness into flame. For in truth, both Hindalom and Milo in their normal Moralian lives were happy and basically kind-hearted. But each had allowed the thorn of violence to grow within him during their stays in the Shadowland, and now both they and their teachers were determined that this sojourn would uproot that evil weed once and for all.

Trillamar stopped speaking, rose, and took his leave of the others in the Apex Room. Jelander waited until his colleague had gone, then said, "let us watch what happened next." The Crystal of Remembrance brightened and the frozen picture began to move again...

FOUR

Hindalom sauntered along with the easy confidence of one who had come this way many times, as they penetrated deeper along the underground passage. The floor was flat for the most part, but at regular intervals a few rough stone steps would lead them down to a new level. As they descended under the earth, the temperature gradually dropped. The air took on a damp, clinging texture and Eluron noticed droplets of water hanging from the rough rock of the walls and ceiling. Here and there small puddles were underfoot.

The tallow candles were set about twenty feet apart along the tunnel. A few had burned down to nothing, leaving darkened stretches in the passageway. At one of these dark regions, Hindalom glanced back over his shoulder and said, "Milo, this is where the accident happened. Do not be afraid. It is in the past."

Milo made no reply, but Eluron noticed that the crippled man was breathing more heavily now, as if some anxiety or fear had gripped him. Hindalom halted briefly at the next wall candle, watching Milo closely as the other hobbled toward him.

"Good," grunted the large man, then turned abruptly to continue along the tunnel.

"How far are we going?" asked Eluron as they negotiated

17

around a large chunk of rock that had fallen from the ceiling.

"Another quarter mile, at most," answered Hindalom. "Is the pace too fast then?"

"I'm alright," replied Eluron, curious now that this giant rough-looking man, who was evidently involved in some unsavory activity, should show such genuine concern — first for Milo and now for him.

At length they came to a widened part in the tunnel, a kind of room with no exit aside from the passage they had just followed and a large stone door mounted on rusty iron hinges. The door was firmly and solidly shut.

"We have to wait here for a few minutes," Hindalom explained. "The door opens by itself when the gatekeeper on the other side moves the lever."

"Why the delay?" asked Eluron. "Can't you knock or something?"

"He is probing this room to see if we are friendly to the Prince or not."

"Probing?"

"The gatekeeper knows what people think," came the unexpected reply.

Eluron fell silent, trying to piece together the adventure into which he had fallen. First there was the initial confrontation with Hindalom and Milo which had promised to end nastily. And then the large man had suddenly taken a liking to Eluron and had now led the three of them to a strange underground ante-room before an imposing stone door behind which someone was 'probing' to find out their feelings about the Prince — whoever that was.

'. . . whoever that was,' Eluron repeated to himself. Then suddenly from some veiled chamber of his memory came a distant recollection. Somehow he knew who — or what — 'the Prince' was. And he knew that where this Prince was, there was great danger.

After a moment, the iron hinges began to creak as the great stone door slowly pivoted open. Standing on the other side was a tall, thin man with large, deep-set eyes — eyes that seemed to pierce through one's very being.

"Two are friendly, the other is neither friend nor enemy," intoned the gatekeeper as he stepped aside to let them pass.

"He will be one of us soon," said Hindalom as Eluron stepped through the doorway and into a completely different chamber. This new room was high and almost perfectly circular with a diameter of about twelve feet. It had wooden benches around its periphery except for the doorway through which they had just stepped, and except for another opening opposite the first. This second portal was unobstructed, and Eluron could see through it to a much more respectable passageway than the rough tunnel they had been following only moments before. This new passage was lined with wood and led off around a gradual curve so that Eluron could see only some thirty feet into it.

Hindalom motioned them to be seated on the benches. Eluron and Milo sat down, while Hindalom began to talk to the gatekeeper in tones too low to allow Eluron to overhear.

About five minutes passed. Hindalom finished his brief conversation with the gatekeeper and sat down at the wall opposite Eluron. The latter shifted uncomfortably as Hindalom peered closely at him.

"I could swear..." muttered the big man, then more loudly he said, "weren't you with us in the last battle?"

"Battle?" Eluron replied.

"I guess not," said Hindalom, and fell silent.

*   *   *

Again the Crystal of Remembrance froze its picture, and the Apex Room brightened slightly. Jelander explained that it was necessary to provide this amount of detail regarding Eluron's adventure in the Shadowland, because Tenuli's main mission during her forthcoming stay in that dark place would be to free Eluron from the situation in which he had become entrapped. And the way she was to accomplish this was to take part in a drama that *reversed*

19

the roles: *she* was to become *physically* entrapped within the Scarlet Castle, and *Eluron* was to be given the opportunity to rescue *her* by rising on the wings of his own courage and resourcefulness — newfound wings that would return to him the inestimable gift of self-respect.

"But what happened to him next?" said Tenuli with wide eyes, so engrossed in the story unfolding in the crystal that she paid scant heed to the implication of danger to herself which Jelander's words carried.

The old teacher smiled at her eagerness. "Little sprite," he said, "it is just that sweet innocence of yours, that childlike quality of excitement, which we hope will rekindle Eluron's memory of his true home here in Moralia. We will pray that you do not lose that endearing trait when we send you in along the Tenth Pathway of Change."

"The Tenth Pathway? What changes does that bring, Jelander?"

"Let us follow Eluron a little further first," he replied, "for then we will be able to show you why the tenth is the only one which will get you close enough to even meet Eluron in his present situation."

* * *

FIVE

Eluron and the other two were now summoned out of the round chamber by a messenger from Korak. They followed the wood-lined tunnel to a large square room which seemed to be in the basement of a normal building. However no windows allowed any light into this space, and Eluron was uncertain just how far underground he was.

The room was even more comfortably appointed than the round chamber had been. There was one large table with a padded armchair behind it, several shelves off to one side with books, a number of racks on which swords and long daggers were mounted, and five chairs facing the table in a semi-circle.

A door opened and three figures entered. The tallest of

20

these was evidently in a position of authority, judging by the obedient glances which the other two cast his way. Eluron, Hindalom and Milo had been sitting in the chairs, and jumped to their feet when the other three entered. The tall man seated himself in the armchair, motioned to his two companions to stand at either end of the table, and then nodded at the others to indicate that they could sit.

Eluron sat down and inspected the figure in the armchair. His clothing was all black, except for a red armband above the left elbow. His dark face had several ugly scars on the left cheek, and another on the right side of the forehead. There was a hint of cruelty around his mouth, and his eyes were sunken below heavy eyebrows that seemed frozen into a permanent frown. His hands were large and rough with thick fingers that were now drumming on the table top.

"I am Korak," said the man, looking at Eluron. "Who are you?" His voice was gruff with a knife-edge of hardness to it.

"Eluron is my name, but I know little else."

"You've just come then," said Korak, "I see."

Hindalom spoke. "We found him at the edge of the city, Korak. I think I know him from somewhere."

Korak looked quickly at Hindalom. "Nonesense. If he has just come, how could you know him?"

"But it seems we were together before," continued Hindalom dubiously, "I don't know..."

"Pure coincidence," said Korak abruptly. "Probably reminds you of someone else. Best forget about it."

Eluron listened closely to this exchange. He sensed that Korak knew something but was trying to prevent Hindalom from finding it out. It was as if Hindalom had almost stumbled upon some sort of truth, and Korak was doing his best to steer him away from it. What secret was Korak hiding? His musing was interrupted by a question directed at Milo.

"How much tonight?" said Korak.

"Over seven hundred. Almost eight hundred," answered the cripple in his thin voice.

"Let's have it then," said Korak, pointing to the table top before him.

Milo took a small bag from the folds of his tunic, hobbled over to the table, and dumped its contents in front of Korak. Out tumbled silver and gold coins, rolling and glinting in the light from the wall torches.

Eluron watched as the coins built a small pile in front of Korak. As the mound grew, he became aware of a strange emotion, an inner prompting — almost like a voice that said, 'you *want* that, Eluron, you *want* that...'

Korak looked up and saw the glint of interest in Eluron's eyes. He leaned back and twisted his mouth into a sardonic smile. "So money attracts you, does it? I see." Then to himself he muttered, "must have come down the second Pathway..."

"Pardon?" said Eluron.

"Never mind," said Korak, staring hard at Eluron's face. He leaned forward, then continued, "Your name was... what?"

"Eluron."

"Hmmm." Korak paused. "Your head shape tells me you are good with figures. Is that right?"

"Uh, I guess... I don't know." Eluron didn't understand the reference to his head shape.

Korak picked up a pencil and scribbled something on a piece of paper. Then he said, "what is 236 plus 79?"

"315."

"How did you get that so fast?"

"I added 80 then took off 1."

"Uh huh... what about 35 times 19?"

Eluron thought a second then said, "665."

"How did you get that?"

"Well, 19 times anything is just 20 times it, minus one of it. 20 times 35 is 700, less 35 leaves 665. Why are you asking me these things?"

"I wanted to see how you handled numbers." Korak gestured to the pile of coins before him. "Do you think you would like to work with... this?"

Eluron's eyes widened as he looked at the mound of

precious metal. "What do you mean?" he asked.

"If you want to have gold and silver around you," replied Korak, "maybe we can arrange that. The Prince needs a new Chief Accountant, someone to keep track of his wealth, control expenditures, and so on. The previous one recently met with... um, an unfortunate accident."

* * *

Tenuli watched the crystal as Eluron eagerly agreed to accept the post which Korak had offered him. Jelander explained that he had taken it because his desire to be around wealth, and to obtain a share of it, was greater than his uneasiness with regard to Korak or his unarticulated fear of 'the Prince'.

Again the picture froze.

"But who *is* Korak?" asked Tenuli, turning to look at Jelander. "Is he from Moralia too?"

"Once long ago Korak walked in this beautiful land," Jelander replied. "But he has brought so much pain to so many in the Shadowland that the evil of his actions prevents him from returning here. You see, each act that brings hurt to someone else casts another layer of darkness over him, and finally he has become so blackened that he could not bear the light and purity of Moralia."

"But is there no way for him to be rid of the darkness?"

"The way is the same for all. It is to pass through the same pain that he inflicted on others. But so much evil has been done that to face it himself would likely destroy him. This he knows, and he has chosen not to embark upon the upward path because it would be too difficult. Instead, he has cast in his lot with the Prince of Shades, and works now to prevent Moralians in the Shadowland from learning their lessons, and from remembering their true homeland."

"How does he know of the Pathways of Change?"

"The Prince of Shades understands well the ways of Moralia, and has explained it all to those who are fully committed to him. That is why Korak recognized Eluron as having likely entered along the Second Pathway. It was he too

23

who appointed Hindalom and Milo to stand at the gate of the Grey City and waylay travellers."

"But why do you not just remove Korak and the Prince from the Shadowland? Have you not the power?"

"Of course that could be done, but it is best to leave things as they are."

"But Korak leads Moralians astray!"

"Only when they themselves allow that to happen. You see, Korak and the rest who serve the Prince of Shades have a very useful function, for they *test* the resolve, the purity and the discernment of those who descend from Moralia to sojourn in that land. Without such testing, we might never be certain that a particular lesson has been truly learned."

"All this talk of lessons is so confusing," Tenuli sighed. "I suppose I shall never know what it means until I arrive in the Shadowland myself."

"Then let us discuss what will happen to you there," said the old teacher.

SIX

Jelander looked closely at Tenuli as he continued. "You will enter the Shadowland along the Tenth Pathway of Change," he said, "which will give you a strong desire to accomplish something important, and the boldness and audacity to carry through your plans. You will have a hard, impudent streak which will co-exist with your natural childlike innocence and charm. Although at times you will wish to be away from the heaviness of the Shadowland, to return to a lighter place you will not completely remember, for the most part the promise of success and importance will lure you and you will forget your secret yearning to be free of that darkened land.

"We will ensure that you, like Eluron, will enter the Shadowland at Sandria, close to the Well of Tears. If you approach the well, you will find that touching the stone wall will not repel you as it did Eluron, because your vib-

24

rations are higher than his and more closely match those of the well itself. It was because of Eluron's melancholy sadness that he found the contact unpleasant.

"Now our hope is that you will drink the well water, for that will keep your memory of Moralia alive longer than usual. Then, whenever you find the memory fading you can return again. However there is a risk that you may not be able to approach the well. The Prince of Shades is planning to destroy it, for he knows that its waters turn Shadowlanders away from allegiance to him. Even now his guards are preventing pilgrims from drawing water."

Jelander continued, explaining that Tenuli would be sent into the Shadowland just before the well was to be visited by a small band of pilgrims — in reality four of the loyal followers of the Knight of Roses. Among these would be Toth, whom Tenuli had known as a good friend in Moralia.

"You will be instantly attracted to Toth," said Jelander, "for not only do you know him well from Moralia, but he was sent in along the Twelfth Pathway of Change, which makes him attractive to those who enter along the tenth or the second. This is caused by the natural compatibility between the changes brought about by these different Pathways. In fact you will feel a stirring of love in a much more personal sense than anything you have known in Moralia, even to the point of wanting to spend all of your time exclusively with him."

"And what will he feel?"

"Toth has passed through the Shadowland many times," replied Jelander. "He will be drawn to you initially, but he will recognize your infatuation as something caused by the other factors I have mentioned. Ultimately he will try to discourage you from feeling that way."

Jelander paused and looked gently at Tenuli. "And that, dear little friend, will be your first taste of pain."

"But how do you know all this will happen? Perhaps Toth and I will just be friends, as we were here in Moralia."

"Yes, that is possible. We cannot fully predict the future, but we know how the Pathways influence Moralians, and we understand the effect of meeting someone previously known here. I am simply explaining the likely course of events."

It was Doran's turn to speak. "There is one more part of the plan," he said, "for I too shall enter the Shadowland, and soon after you. We shall not meet there until after you have been caused pain by Toth, but when at last our paths cross, you will find a more enduring and balanced friendship than Toth could have given you."

Tenuli put her hand in his and looked at him with such pure affection in her eyes that Doran was grieved at his inability to return her devotion measure for measure. He knew how attached Tenuli was to him, and it pained him to realize that he could not love as she did. Yet he had great compassion for her, and his heart tightened at the thought of the hurt she would soon suffer at the hands of Toth.

"Dear little sprite . . . " he began softly, then stopped as tears of chagrin came to his eyes.

Jelander decided to bring the discussion back to the matter at hand. "Well," he said, "we must make plans. Anyway, it is best that you should not understand too much of Doran's role in the adventure ahead, for if you knew that he would find you one day, your attraction to Toth might be weakened. This makes it necessary for us to wipe your memory clean regarding Doran, so that even when you drink from the Well of Tears, you will not remember him. When it is time for you both to meet, we will allow your memory to return."

Tenuli was silent for a long moment. Then she took a deep breath and said, "I am ready."

* * *

SEVEN

The horses were tired. Toth looked back at his three companions and signalled with his hand to pull up and dismount. It was late, and they had to pitch camp before the dim half-light of daytime deepened to the inky impenetrable blackness of night in the land of shadows.

Fromil and Sindor dismounted and began to collect wood for a fire. Toth and the fourth man, whom they called the Silent One, watered and fed the horses.

Tall, slim, nordic — Toth had the kind of face that painters and sculptors dream of: chiseled features, a fine, straight nose, flaxen blond hair, and cornflower blue eyes that could see clear through to the other side of any question or any person. Soon after his arrival in the Shadowland Toth had encountered the Silent One, whom he had instantly liked and trusted, and who had taken him to the Redwood Forest to join the followers of the Knight of Roses. Toth had quickly demonstrated his leadership qualities, and the Knight had soon asked him to become his informal second-in-command.

By regularly tasting the water from the Well of Tears, Toth had managed to keep alive the flame of his memory and love for Moralia — not the details, not specific names and events, but a sure conviction that the Shadowland was indeed a land of shades and illusion, and that his mission was to help banish that darkness forever by working to defeat the Prince of Shades.

As always at this time of day, Toth's mind stirred with wraith-like memories of Moralia, and the knowledge that in his real homeland not only was the daylight far brighter than the dismal illumination of this shadowed place, but by some wonder of design it continued unbroken by nightfall, a continual effulgence of clarity and warmth that bathed everyone and everything in a limitless sea of magical light.

When the fire had been lit and the cheery flames were licking up along the blackened sides of the little pot, they sat down in a semi-circle around the warm glow, listening to the wood snap and hiss, staring into the red embers at the base of the fire.

"A good day's journey," said Toth. "Tomorrow we arrive at Sandria, just before nightfall."

Fromil poked at the fire with a stick. "Wonder if we'll find any of the Prince's men hanging around. You've heard the talk too, I think — that he's laid his evil plans to destroy the Well of Tears."

"Just a rumour," came the voice of Sindor. "He wouldn't dare to attack the well. There's too many here in Shadowland that would rise up against him if he did."

"Maybe not enough," said Toth slowly, "maybe not enough. Besides, he knows that if he can just keep people away from the well for a few months, everyone will forget about it. Even you, Sindor, would cease to recall the beautiful land we came from, without the water from the Well of Tears."

Sindor stared gloomily into the fire. "Perhaps," he said. "Anyway, if we do meet with any of the Prince's men, I swear they'll remember the day as the unluckiest they've seen."

"No," said Toth. "The violent way is *their* way. If we too should fight except in self-defense, we can never hope to win them over to our side. The Knight of Roses has explained it all to you: that our secret weapon is not the sword or the dagger; it is the water from the Well of Tears. If we can get the Prince's men to taste that magical liquid, most of them will quickly remember their true purpose here in the land of shadows, and we will be able to persuade them to turn against the Prince and join us. Remember that most of the Prince's men — except for a few like Korak — were once our friends in Moralia. Our task is not to destroy them, for that is exactly what the evil Prince wants to happen — destruction on all sides. *We* are fighting a *different* kind of battle — a battle of persuasion. Our victories are not measured in the number of soldiers we can destroy, but in the number of sleeping memories we can awaken."

The others did not reply.

They shared the meager meal in the little pot, then watched in silence as the fire faded to a few red embers — each one lost in his own thoughts.

Toth stirred in his sleep. The cold ground dug into his ribs as he shifted to find a more comfortable sleeping position.

He stirred again, not able to escape the protrusion under him. Then he sat up and looked over at the others. Fromil and Sindor were fast asleep, but the Silent One was sitting on the other side of the fire — now just a dull red glow — looking up at something above him. He had not heard Toth stir, but he did catch the movement from the corner of his eye and turned to smile. Then he pointed up at an angle, and made a sign with his other hand that meant 'messenger'.

Toth looked up into the sky — a sky which he had fully expected to be solid black as it always was. But suddenly he saw what the Silent One was pointing at — a tiny pin-prick of blue-white, shining steadily against the darkness of the sky, a single dot of light in the black mantle that shrouded their world. He, like everyone in Shadowland, knew the legend of Sandria, but that story told of a bigger circle of brilliant light so bright that nobody could look at it. Not a tiny spot like this.

Again the Silent One made the sign for 'messenger' with his hand. Toth signalled back, 'messenger of what?' The Silent One glanced up again at the dot of light, then he said with his hands, 'a great thing comes soon.' 'A portent,' thought Toth. 'He thinks it foretells an important event.' Toth was aware of the abilities of the Silent One, who often knew things before they happened, and could tell just by looking at a person whether he was a follower of the Prince or not. Now Toth wondered whether again the Silent One was right. Certainly, Toth knew of no stories about little dots of light like this one. Perhaps it *was* an omen of something to come. He looked up again... the dot was gone! Toth looked around in a larger circle — maybe it had moved. But it was not to be seen. He looked at the Silent One and raised his eyebrows in question. The other simply shrugged, then again made the sign for 'messenger'.

Lost in thought, Toth lay down again, squirmed to find a position in harmony with the unfriendly ground, and gradually drifted into a fitful sleep.

The next morning, the band of pilgrims rose early, broke camp, mounted up and began the day's journey. Toth described the tiny spot of light to Fromil and Sindor, and together they discussed what it might have been. But they came to no conclusion, for nobody in the Shadowland had ever seen a star before that night...

The day passed uneventfully. As evening approached, the pilgrims caught sight of the tall steeple of Sandria, rising above the dull tree line.

"We must be careful now," said Toth. "Fromil could be right about the Prince's men. If they are around, they might well suspect that we are followers of the Knight of Roses and attack. Remember that our best weapon is not our sword, but the well water in our pouches. Try to aim some of it into the face of anyone who attacks you. If it touches his lips, he will remember the truth." Toth looked at Sindor. "They are your brothers, Sindor," he said, "brothers who have forgotten their kinship with us. You have still much anger against any who have sided with the Prince. But your anger plays right into his hands, for it pits Shadowlanders against Shadowlanders — and that is just what the Prince wants. Secretly he cares nothing for those who serve him, and wishes to destroy them as well as us. Remember what the Knight of Roses has taught — to open our hearts to them, to feel affection even for the ones who seem to hate us. If we can do that, then the Prince will be powerless against us."

"How can I feel love for one who hates me?" asked Sindor. "It's unnatural. If they want a fight, I say give them a bloody good one!"

Toth sighed and said nothing. He remembered how Sindor's best friend had been cruelly tortured by the Prince's jailers in the dungeons under the Scarlet Castle, and wondered how he himself might have reacted in Sindor's place.

They pulled the horses up behind a clump of trees some five hundred yards from the edge of Sandria. In the distance they could perceive the outline of the Well of Tears,

and noted two men standing near the circular wall around
the well.

"They're not drinking or looking into it," said Fromil,
"they've got their backs to it."

"The bloody Prince's men, I'll swear to it," said Sindor.

Toth put a finger to his lips. "As quietly as you can now,"
he said. "We'll tether the horses here, then one by one
we'll walk up to that tall grey building by the square where
the well is. We cannot go together, for if they *are* with the
Prince they will suspect us. I'll be first; Fromil you're
second. Sindor will go third and the Silent One last."

The Silent One reached over and tugged at Toth's sleeve.
He pointed at the well and then signalled 'Prince' with his
hands.

Toth said, "the Prince's men?" The other nodded.

"Remember your pouch, Sindor," he said, then moved
out from behind the trees and began walking casually
toward Sandria.

EIGHT

Tenuli's head was spinning. A moment before she had
been gazing into the dear faces of Jelander and Doran, and
now the faces were gone and she found herself on the
ground beside a tall building of grey brick under a leaden
sky.

She knew she must remember something, but what was it?
Oh, if only her head were not spinning so! Wait... yes!
That was it! *Moralia*... and Jelander her teacher, and
Doran her friend, and... and... Elur–,El–

Like a dream that ghostily fades in the morning light, her
memory of Moralia was slipping away from her. She sat
up and rubbed her eyes, looking around to get her bearings. A short distance away she saw the circular stone wall
of a little water well, and two heavy-set men standing
nearby with their backs to it.

The sight of the well jogged something in the 'dream' she
now only vaguely remembered ... something about going

31

to it and drinking the water. Shakily she got to her feet, steadying herself against the wall of the building.

A beautiful voice from behind her said, "are you alright, Miss?"

She turned and looked straight into the friendliest, twinklingest blue eyes she had ever seen. "Oh," she said, "I, uh..."

"You look a little unsteady," said Toth, taking a step forward to support her arm.

"Thank you," said Tenuli, smiling shyly at the blond stranger. "I'm not sure where I am..."

"No memory of this place?"

"It seems strange — as if I should be somewhere else..."

"Then you have just come," said Toth. "Do you not recognize the Well of Tears yonder?"

"I know I must drink from it," she replied.

"Yes," he said, "it will help you to remember where you have come from. But I fear that drinking from the well may not be a simple matter. It looks as if those guards mean to keep everyone away from it."

Toth reached into his tunic and drew out the water pouch. "Here," he said, "this contains some of the well water. It was drawn over two months ago and has lost much of its potency, but it should help you somewhat." He opened the pouch and held it for her as she drank.

"Yes," she said as fragments of her life in Moralia came back to her memory. "I can recall vaguely, but it is more like a remembered dream than a reality."

"From the Shadowland, it always seems merely a dream," he replied. "But when you are there, in that beautiful, summery, shining land, you know that *this* is the dream world, that *here* is the place of illusions."

"My name is Tenuli," she said, "but who are you? I recognize something about you, but I am still very confused."

"I am Toth," he said simply. "I am a follower of the Knight of Roses and we—"

"What?" she said suddenly. "Why, I think I know about him. Is he not seeking to make this place more like the

32

beautiful land that the water has made me remember?"

"Yes," he replied. "We wish to bring the light of Moralia into the Shadowland."

"Moralia!" she cried. "Yes! That is the name of my home. Oh, how beautiful it was!"

"We believe that the beauty of Moralia can be here as well," said Toth. Then he looked over at the two guards near the well and continued softly, "but we must bring about the changes ourselves. This darkness comes from within the hearts of Shadowlanders. Remove it first from there, and this land would soon be flooded with light."

By now the other three had reached the edge of Sandria, and were standing together a little distance from Toth and Tenuli. Toth turned and saw them, glanced again at the guards near the Well of Tears, then said softly to Tenuli, "best to move back to where my friends are standing yonder. One of us can stay with you while the others attempt to obtain some of the water from the Well of Tears. We need it in our work for the Knight of Roses, and I think you should drink some of it fresh from the well. It will bring your memory back more clearly."

They bent low and moved back to where the others were standing. After some discussion it was decided that Sindor would stay with Tenuli, and that the other three would tackle the guards. The plan was for Toth to stroll casually up to the well and begin talking with one of them. He would use some pretense to persuade the guard to look down into the well since that would have a stronger effect than contact with the two-month-old water in Toth's pouch. Meanwhile Fromil and the Silent One would position themselves at opposite sides of the square, appearing to be relaxing under the trees, so that they could rush in to help if Toth got into trouble.

Since they did not know how the guards would react to Toth's approach, they did not plan any further than that. As events unfolded, they would simply take whatever action was appropriate. If all else failed, then as a last resort they would try to dash some of their pouch water into the guards' faces. They hoped that it would confuse

33

them long enough to allow the Silent One — who was the strongest of the four — to draw several pails of water from the well and fill a large water bag which he carried under his tunic.

They shook hands all together, and then Toth, Fromil and the Silent One set off in different directions. Tenuli and Sindor crouched under some bushes and watched.

Toth ambled across the square toward the Well of Tears. The nearer guard saw him and held up his hand. "Sorry," he said, "no water today!"

Toth stopped and smiled his most disarming smile. "They've closed it up?" he asked, "filled it in?"

"Don't know about filled in," said the guard, "just have orders from the Prince that nobody draws water until further notice."

"Well, if it's been filled in, I sure hope they got all of the gold coins out of the bottom first..."

There was a pause.

"Gold coins?"

"You don't know about the gold coins in the well?"

"What gold coins?"

"I met a man two days travel from here, who said he'd managed to pull up more than two dozen coins from the bottom of the well, and that there were hundreds more still there. Said you could see the coins at the bottom if you looked carefully..."

"Orders are not to look into the well," said the guard gruffly, but he turned and glanced over at the wall of the well about twenty feet away.

Toth tried to sound casual. "The man I met said he just smeared some pine gum on a rock and lowered it down on a long string — and up came all these coins. Tell you what: if you'll help me get some gum from that tree yonder, we'll use a string that I've brought and I'll split whatever comes up fifty-fifty with you."

"Not supposed to leave the well," said the guard, then added, "...though I don't imagine a couple of minutes would hurt...what tree?"

"At the edge of the square. There." Toth pointed to a

large pine tree near where Fromil was standing.

The guard hesitated. "Just a minute," he said. "How do I know this isn't some trick? Maybe you're a follower of the Knight of Roses, just trying to get me to look down the well. They say the well is enchanted — confuses people who look into it, makes them change."

Toth laughed. "You believe those old tales? Well, I'll bet it won't change *me*," he said. "Here I'll prove it to you."

Before the guard could stop him. Toth stepped to the side of the well, and looked down at his reflection in the still water. Instantly his mind flooded again with the sure knowledge of his home in Moralia. He saw the face of his teacher, and for a brief second recognized the Moralian identity of the guard with whom he had been talking. They had been students together in one of Trillamar's classes in the Temple of Learning.

Toth straightened up, struggling not to show any change to the guard. "There," he smiled, "nothing to it. All I saw was the glint of gold under the water. Here, have a look for yourself."

The guard's curiosity was by now too much for him to withstand. Glancing over at the other guard to ensure that his back was turned, he sidestepped his way over to the Well of Tears. Then he shaded his eyes, and quickly bent to look down into the water.

"I don't see any gold co—" Suddenly he stopped speaking and straightened up, a totally bewildered look on his face. "No," he said softly, "these pictures…"

The other guard turned and saw what was happening. "Hey!" he shouted, and began running toward them, drawing his sword. Toth backstepped away from him, reaching into his tunic for the pouch of well water. At the same instant Fromil and the Silent One began running full tilt toward them from opposite sides of the square. Further away, Sindor stood up, drawing his dagger.

The next few seconds were a blur. Toth unstopped the pouch and aimed it. The second guard slashed toward him with his sword, nicking Toth's left arm and making a neat slice right through the pouch. The water spilled out as Toth danced sideways to avoid the next swing of the sword-edge. He tripped on a rock and fell heavily to the ground. The guard raised his sword again to deliver the death stroke — and that's when the Silent One hit him from behind, wrapping his powerful arms around the man's chest, squeezing and lifting. The sword clattered harmlessly to the ground.

"Take him to the well!" shouted Fromil, at the same time helping Toth to his feet. "Make him look in!"

The silent One moved quickly to the well and forced the guard over the edge, pushing his head down toward the water.

"No!" shouted the guard. "I will not look!"

"Tie him, then," said Toth, holding his left arm to stop the bleeding. "Fromil, use the cord here in my tunic." Then he signalled to the Silent One to fill the large bag with well water as quickly as possible. "Hurry," he said, "there may be other guards around."

"What about the first guard?" asked Fromil, nodding over to where the latter was sitting holding his head and mumbling to himself.

"Give him some fresh well water to drink," answered Toth. "His name is Blenik. I knew him as a friend in Moralia. He will remember it all and join us."

After the second guard had been securely tied, Fromil filled his own pouch with freshly drawn water and then approached Blenik. "Here," he said gently, "this will help clear your head." The confused man lifted the pouch to his lips and drank. "Do you remember?" asked Fromil.

"Yes," said the other. "I remember enough to make me ashamed of what I have been doing here in the Shadowland."

Toth had come over and now sat down opposite Blenik. "Do not be hard on yourself," he said softly. "When we come to the land of shadows we are all changed, and sometimes the changes bring pressures and temptations that are hard to withstand. By yielding to them first and then later seeing the truth, we often learn the lessons more surely.

36

We come here to experience darkness, for it teaches us to cherish the light."

"Thank you," said Blenik. Tears were in his eyes. "Thank you, my friend Toth."

"Come with us," said Toth. "You cannot now continue as you were. The other guard knows you have looked into the well. It is too dangerous for you to remain here."

They helped Blenik to his feet, and moved off to where Sindor and Tenuli were waiting. The Silent One carried the large water bag on his shoulder, as it was too heavy for any of the others to lift.

NINE

"Your arm!" cried Tenuli. "You're wounded!"

"Just a nick," smiled Toth, waving his left arm about to show that the cut was not serious.

The Silent One set down the large water bag and detached a small container of red powder from his belt. Then he knelt and sprinkled it on the sword-wound. Instantly the bleeding stopped.

"What is that powder?" asked Tenuli.

"Cayenne Pepper," replied Toth. "It stops bleeding. Thank you, friend." He nodded at the Silent One. Then he looked around at the others and said, "we must not tarry in this place. Sandria will be crawling with the Prince's men by daybreak. We'll ride to a place I know about five miles from here. There are two small hunting cabins that should be unoccupied. We can lay over there until the excitement we've caused dies down."

They walked quickly to where the horses were tethered, mounted up, and rode away from Sandria as the dim light of day began to deepen toward the inky blackness of nighttime in the land of shadows..

Toth rode ahead, with Tenuli sitting on the saddle behind him. They talked and laughed, discovering that they had much in common. Because both had drunk some of the fresh well water, they each felt the same easy familiarity

37

with the other — a familiarity based on shared experiences in Moralia. But Tenuli sensed that her friendship for this brave, blue-eyed young man was fast blossoming into something more. She tightened her grip about his waist as the horse shifted to avoid an obstacle, and she discovered how pleasant it was to have her arms around him. Toth too was keenly aware of how this trusting, wide-eyed girl made him feel.

By the time they had covered half the distance to the abandoned cabins, Tenuli had made up her mind that she wanted to be with Toth from now on, and she decided to make him feel the same way. She had fallen in love, without even realizing it had happened.

This feeling of fluttery excitement was wholly new to little Tenuli. There had been many friends whom she dearly loved in Moralia, but never with the same pressure in the heart that she felt now. Glancing around at the little band of men following behind, she realized that Toth's loyalty to them and to this Knight of Roses might interfere with her desire to spend all of her time with him. Suddenly she became jealous of these demands upon Toth, and she determined to find out how serious he was about his other loyalties.

"Toth," she said coyly, "do you have to give *all* your efforts to the Knight of Roses? Do you not sometimes yearn to be free? To do what you want?"

"But I *am* free, Tenuli," he replied. "We are not bound to the Knight by fear or duty, but by love for what he is seeking to accomplish. I could leave this service to him whenever I wished. But I have made a promise to *myself* that I will not rest until the evil Prince of Shades has been driven out or destroyed, and the light of Moralia has been brought to the land of shadows. For then all of us will be free to follow our hearts and discover the beauty which now lies hidden under this cloak of darkness that covers Shadowland."

His eloquence touched a chord of truth within her, but she fought to subdue that recognition for the sake of the infatuation that had invaded her heart. She made a pout with her lips. "Sometimes you sound like you are reading from a book," she said petulently.

Toth chuckled deep in his throat. "In a way," he replied, "I am. Whenever the words flow like that, it is because my teacher has touched my thought. Often it is *his* words that I speak, not my own."

"You mean the Knight of Roses?"

"No, though he too is a wonderful teacher. I meant my teacher in Moralia."

Tenuli fell silent, not knowing how to deal with the point of view that Toth was expressing. Though the well water had made her remember Moralia and Jelander, her infatuation was forcing her to ignore that knowledge. She decided to be more forthright, and to find out whether Toth felt the same as she.

"Toth," she began, "I am so happy that you found me in Sandria."

"Yes, you could have been picked up by those guards, and who knows what might have become of you?"

"No, I mean I am glad it was *you* that found me. I feel so...happy when I am near you."

Toth realized where the discussion was heading. "Tenuli," he said, "we have been friends in Moralia, and this always brings two people closer than otherwise. But I have much to accomplish here in the Shadowland. Do not fear. The Knight's followers will take good care of you, and I shall always be at your call whenever you need a special friend."

With a pang she knew that Toth did not feel as she did. Her heart felt constricted, as if someone were squeezing it between his hands. Her face burning with humiliation, she fought to keep the tears back...and lost. Toth turned sideways and put his arm around the sobbing girl.

"Dear Tenuli," he said, "forgive me. I would not willingly hurt you. But my loyalty calls me away into dangerous places where you cannot go. It is best that we remain friends, for that we have always been."

She said nothing for the remainder of the trip. Toth felt responsible for Tenuli's pain, but he could think of nothing that would comfort her, so he too remained silent.

By the time they arrived at the hunting cabins, Tenuli's humiliation had hardened into a resolve to do something that would make Toth look at her as more than just an innocent little girl who 'couldn't follow him into danger'. Part of her wanted to hurt him as he had hurt her — to 'get even'. Another part, the part that loved Toth, wanted to help him destroy the Prince of Shades. Still another, the humiliated part, wanted to 'show him' by going right into the most dangerous place in the land of shadows — just so he would see that she was no innocent babe in the woods.

She was given a private room in one of the crude cabins, which Toth's men tried to fix up as comfortably as possible. As she lay on the rough bunk with silent tears in her eyes, a plan gradually formed in her mind — a plan that would lead her into the very teeth of the storm that was brewing in Shadowland, and would plunge her into the greatest battle ever fought between the forces of good and the forces of evil.

* * *

In Moralia, Jelander smiled. "It is all happening as we planned, Doran," he said. "Soon it will be your turn to go."

TEN

Now it is important to understand that the water from the Well of Tears did not affect *all* Shadowlanders in exactly the same way. The effect it had depended greatly upon just how far into the shadows one had descended. If a person had resisted many of the temptations of the darker world, and refused to give in to cruelty or greed or selfishness, then that person would always find that the well water produced an immediate recollection of his true home in Moralia, and allowed him to recognize many of his acquaintances of Shadowland in their true Moralian

40

identities. The experience, for one such as this, was always a joyous one. That is how the water affected Toth, for example, who had managed to remain true to his best self despite the pervading melancholy which the Twelfth Pathway of Change tended to impose upon those who had selected that route of entry into the Shadowland.

Toth had drunk from the well many times, and had now a permanent awareness of the truth of Moralia and the fact that the Shadowland was only a temporary abode where people came to learn things at an accelerated pace. But it required many repeated experiences of the water's effect, as well as a determination to retain the truth, in order to arrive at that strength of conviction. If a person were to drink from the Well of Tears only once, he would find that the vision it produced soon faded, like the fragments of a half-remembered dream. Unless a sincere effort were made to hang on to the memory, it was soon replaced by the normal everyday point of view. Tenuli herself, despite her unspoiled inner purity, was experiencing this struggle between the awareness which the well water gave and the self-oriented attitude which came from a combination of the Tenth Pathway and the hurt which she had just experienced.

The degree to which one had developed the darker tendencies in himself also influenced the effect which the well water had. Blenik, for example, had partly given in to the temptations of the lower world and had yielded to the darker shades which his Pathway of Change had impressed upon him. In his case, the well water had to combat ingrained habits of a shadowy kind — mainly meanness and greed — and this fight between truth and darkness produced a sense of confusion and bewilderment at first.

Eluron too was in this middle category. He had not looked into or drunk from the Well of Tears, but had merely touched the wet stones of its wall. Yet this contact seemed unpleasant to him, because of the contrast between the purity of the Well of Tears and the darker shades of Eluron's morose and covetous nature.

Then there were the ones who were so far gone in their

evil habits that the well water — if ever they dared even to touch it — would produce a searing, burning heat that would be the worst pain they could possibly endure. For this reason Korak, and others like him, stayed very far away from the Well of Tears. In fact, the vast gulf between the high, pure vibrations of the well and the base, mean vibrations of people like Korak made it impossible for them to approach Sandria any closer than about one mile. It was just too uncomfortable for them to get any nearer.

It will now be clear, perhaps, why Toth did not force the second guard — the one who attacked him — to drink any of the water from the well. Toth knew about the pain that the water could cause in those who had shifted too far toward evil, and he judged from the violent nature of the second guard and his refusal to open his eyes and look into the well, that it would be cruel to subject the man to such discomfort.

The Knight of Roses had often cautioned his followers against the indiscriminate use of the well water. "Remember," he would say, "many of your brothers cannot face the sudden shock of truth which the water brings. The realization that they have lost their way and disappointed their teachers can cause much confusion and pain. Use the water wisely, just as you do your words. For those who are not receptive, neither the spoken truth nor the pure revelations of the Well of Tears are appropriate. Indeed, to force truth upon one not yet able to perceive it may simply drive him further away from the light. And that is not what we are about."

Having explained this very important point about the Well of Tears, we may now return to the little hunting cabins and look in upon Tenuli and the others.

Tenuli had spent a fitful night — alternately sleeping and waking, crying and plotting. By morning her plan was firmly laid, and she awaited only the opportunity to act. She had recognized during the night that she did not hate Toth, and that she merely resented the humiliation he had caused her. Indeed, her attraction to this strange young man was undiminished, and part of her plan was to make him respect and admire her so that one day he would feel as she did.

She took control of her emotions, surprising herself that she could so readily do this, and pretended to have 'got over' the scene of the day before. Toth, wise beyond his years, knew that she was hiding her disappointment. But he made no reference to the previous day's events.

When they had finished the morning meal, Toth assembled them together. "By tomorrow it should be safe to return to the stronghold of the Knight of Roses," he said. "Today we should venture out only to gather firewood and whatever berries can be found. This place is but a day's ride from the Scarlet Castle, along this same road. We must post a look-out, so that we can be warned if any of the Prince's men happen along. Fromil, Sindor and I will forage in the nearby woods, and the Silent One will stay to protect Tenuli. Blenik, you head up the road and watch for riders coming from the castle. There is a hill about twenty minutes ride away. From there, you can see a good two miles up the road, without yourself being visible."

They all agreed, and after the breakfast things had been cleaned and packed for an instant escape if need be, they set out upon their separate tasks.

Tenuli had listened carefully to the discussion and Toth's directions. From what he had said, she concluded that if she could get away unnoticed on one of the horses, she could reach the Scarlet Castle by nightfall. However Blenik and the Silent One presented a problem. She decided that the best way to escape would be to persuade the Silent One to let her go out on her own to pick berries close to the cabins. If she could then slip away into the woods and follow along parallel to the road, she might be able to take Blenik's horse without him noticing right away. It would take Blenik a good hour to walk back along the road he had ridden in twenty minutes, and that should give her enough of a lead to reach the castle before they overtook her. In any event she doubted whether Toth would put his men at risk by chasing her all the way, since he would conclude that she was quite determined to reach the castle.

After the three foragers had departed, and Blenik had mounted one of the four horses and ridden off, she tried to make herself understood by the Silent One, performing elaborate gestures to represent the door opening and herself picking berries. Smiling, the Silent One pointed to his lips and moved them as if in speech, indicating that he could lip-read. Embarassed, she explained her wish in words and was relieved to find him agreeing readily. Still smiling, he opened the door for her. Then he cupped his hand over his ear, which she took to indicate that she should listen to the sounds around her, and return if danger threatened. As she was leaving, he reached for one of the full water pouches and placed it into her hands, licking his lips to simulate thirst. Gratefully she took the pouch and slung the strap over her shoulder.

Then the door closed and she was alone outside the cabin. She took a moment to get her bearings, calculated where she should enter the woods in order to strike a path parallel to the road, and then set off. Yet her mind lingered on that curious smile of the Silent One. It made her feel as if he had known all about her plan. But that was impossible of course...or was it?

For a while she fought her way through the underbrush parallel to the road, snapping twigs, swishing branches and making muffled cries as brambles scraped her arms. After ten minutes of this noisy, painful progress, she decided that she might as well walk on the road, since Blenik would surely hear her blundering through the brush this way. If she was lucky he would be facing the other way and she would see him before he caught sight of her.

* * *

"She is approaching Blenik," said Jelander to Trillamar. "We must ensure that he does not see her before she can take his horse. Her mission requires her to meet Eluron in the Scarlet Castle, and this point in her path is one where

44

chance could prevent her escape. We must concentrate on Blenik's mind, lulling it so that he will not notice Tenuli's approach."

Trillamar studied the picture in the Crystal of Forever. "He is my student," he replied, "and his thought process is more akin to mine than to yours. I will project the energy, if you will link and give me the extra power."

The wise teachers concentrated.

* * *

Blenik's mind seemed to glaze over as he sat staring along the road to the castle. For a few minutes it was as if he had entered that half-world between waking and sleeping. And it was just then that Tenuli caught sight of his horse, tethered a short distance off the road. A second later she saw Blenik's back over the ridge of the hill where he was sitting. Stealthily she crept up to the horse, making sure the animal could see her. She did not want to startle the beast. Her left hand gently stroked his nose as she undid the tether with her right. Then she led him out to the roadway, mounted and spurred him to a full gallop in the direction of the Scarlet Castle.

She hardly heard Blenik's shout of surprise for the pounding of the horse's hooves.

The first phase of her plan had been a success.

ELEVEN

Tenuli slowed her horse to an easier pace, for she sensed that the animal was tiring. She had been riding for almost two hours along the road and she too was becoming fatigued. Off to the left she noticed a small stream, and decided to pull up and allow the horse to drink.

She dismounted and held the bridle as she led the animal away from the road toward the gentle babbling of the little stream. She found a convenient location where the water tumbled over a small rocky bed, and bent to splash some of the cool wetness on her face as the horse drank.

Tenuli was more tired than she had thought, and decided to sit and rest for a few moments. She did not know why, but being near this little brook was very pleasant, as if it reminded her of other happy experiences which she could not quite recall. She seemed to sense that it was possible to 'understand' the voice of the water, although she did not know where that notion came from. For Tenuli, who had drunk only once from the Well of Tears, the truth of Moralia had now faded to a filmy, blurred image that she could not easily pull back into her conscious mind.

As she sat resting, the continual murmur of the little brook lulled her into a state half awake and half asleep. In that condition of quiet reverie, a picture gradually formed itself before her inner sight. The picture was of a great pyramid covered in gold on the two sides she could see. Standing on the wide alabaster steps leading to the entranceway was a tall robed figure with a kindly face and twinkling eyes. The murmur of the little brook in the background seemed to change and blend into the words which the robed figure was saying: "Tuli," came the gentle voice, "remember that you are not of this shadowy place, that your true home is where the light shines from everywhere to everywhere. Many trials await you here, and these are sent to test your innate goodness. Whenever you are in doubt about the best course to follow, whenever the darkness seems to hide the truth from you, fasten your attention on the Great Light that is within and around you, for it shall never fail. And when you need a friend with whom you can share the secrets of your joy and your sorrow, seek out the sound of a running stream as you have done here, and close your eyes. I will talk to you through the voice of the waters."

"But who are you?" she framed the question in her mind.

"I am one who watches over you," came the reply.

And the little stream babbled on.

Suddenly Tenuli opened her eyes. 'Oh dear,' she thought, 'how long have I been here?' She glanced around and was relieved to see the horse still standing quietly by the stream. Not knowing whether minutes or hours had passed, she arose quickly and led the animal back to the road. Then she mounted and resumed her journey.

'What a strange dream I had,' she thought to herself. 'The kind man by the pyramid seemed to be a friend, yet I don't recall having known him before.'

She decided to think no more about the curious encounter, and instead concentrated on her plan. She had heard Toth and the others speaking of one called Korak, who she gathered was a close lieutenant of the Prince of Shades himself. From their remarks, she realized that Korak was a particularly evil man. Shivering at the thought of exposing herself to his dark presence, she tried not to concentrate on the danger that every passing minute brought closer.

*   *   *

In Moralia, Jelander noted her thoughts and nodded. "She has much courage, Trillamar," he said, "and a short while ago she did not even know what courage was."

"Yes," replied Trillamar, "how quickly the Shadowland allows us to see what qualities lie within the hearts of Moralians."

"We were right to choose the Tenth Pathway of Change," mused Jelander. "Her plan stems partly from the audacity which that ray inspires."

"And the pain of lost love has triggered it all," replied the other. "In the end, that pain will have bestowed upon her a great gift — the gift of knowing herself more deeply."

*   *   *

TWELVE

Hours later, Tenuli began to notice that the countryside was becoming rougher and rockier. Growing things were now more and more sparse, and the few scattered trees seemed gnarled and stunted. It was as if something nearby were choking off the life-force of all vegetation, making it struggle for a foot-hold in this inimical landscape — a suffocating weight that pressed down upon every living thing with a brooding heaviness.

Tenuli herself felt this leaden presence in the air, for her heart seemed burdened with a melancholy foreboding that she had not before experienced. As she crested a small hill in the road, her eyes fell upon the thing which was causing both the feeling in her heart and the stunted growth around her: high on its outcropping of veined grey rock stood the Scarlet Castle, its stones a deep blood-red, its menacing outline etched against the dull sky. A bolt of fear went through her as she pulled the horse to a stop, and her body began to shake uncontrollably.

For it is one thing to sit in the warmth and comfort of Moralia and listen to your kind teacher describe the Scarlet Castle; but it is quite another thing to find yourself alone and unprotected before this monstrous evil structure, with nowhere to go but straight into the jaws of the nameless dangers that lurked within its forbidding walls. It is no wonder that poor little Tenuli was terrified.

Yet from some deep well within her being she managed to draw forth the self-control she needed, and calmed herself down. Again she surprised herself by so quickly taking charge of her roiled emotions, not realizing that this quality was a gift from the Tenth Pathway of Change.

She set her chin, determined not to be intimidated by the appearance of the castle, and spurred her horse toward the evil outline that loomed ahead.

High in one of the turrets, Korak moved in his chair. He had been instructed by the Prince of Shades to wait in this upper chamber and watch the road from the west. The Prince had said that a lone woman traveller would soon approach the castle, and had ordered that she be taken in and given a comfortable room. He had also directed Korak to meet with the woman the following morning, and offer her a position with the staff of the castle. That meant that Korak would have to appear pleasant, and he deeply resented having to be pleasant to anyone — especially a woman.

Now his eyes caught the movement of something on the road, and he heard the steady clip-clop of horse's hooves. Quickly he summoned two of his guards and instructed them to approach the traveller. "If it is a woman," he said, "do not warn her away. Instead tell her that the Prince is hospitable to strangers and invite her to spend the night here. Pretend you are friendly. She is to have the orange room in the east wing."

The guards went immediately to carry out their orders.

Tenuli was still half a mile away when she saw the main castle gate open, and two mounted figures ride through it toward her. Fearfully she continued forward to meet them, hoping that when they saw she was a woman and unarmed, they would not attack.

"Pull up!" shouted one of the guards as he approached her. Then, seeing Tenuli, he continued in a pleasanter tone, "we have been commanded to accompany you, Miss. The Prince is friendly to travellers, and bids you welcome to the Scarlet Castle. Please follow us."

Surprised at this turn of events, Tenuli thanked them, and proceeded behind them toward the still open gate of the castle.

They entered the foreyard and she dismounted. The guards then led her through an enormous hall hung with tapestries which depicted battle scenes in dull colours, echos of ancient wars and forgotten campaigns frozen forever in the heavy, dyed threads. She followed them along a dimly lit corridor, and up a wide staircase to a second-storey room decorated with orange draperies and rugs.

"This is where you will sleep," said the guard. "Korak will see you in the morning."

The name of Korak made her heart jump, but she pretended it had no effect on her. When the door had closed behind the guards, she fell exhausted into bed. Her mind noted with surprise how comfortable the bed was, but any subsequent musings were dissolved away in the ocean of sleep that soon engulfed her.

49

The next day she was awakened by a sharp rap at the door. She jumped out of bed and her eyes fell on a clean outfit of clothing neatly laid upon a nearby table. Tenuli did not remember seeing these clothes the night before, but assumed she must have been too tired to notice. Quickly she donned the fresh apparel, then walked to the door and opened it.

The face of the man standing in the corridor was strangely familiar to Tenuli, and she experienced the kind of odd recognition that one might feel upon discovering in the attic a faded photograph of some childhood friend not heard from in many years.

"I am Eluron," said the man, "please follow me. Korak will see you now."

Eluron! Why was that name so familiar? The shock of seeing this known but unknown person was such that she could think of no words to answer him with. Obediently she followed as he turned on his heels and strode off down the corridor.

The meeting with Korak was remarkable, in that the roles one might have expected those present to play were strangely interchanged. Korak did his best to appear pleasant, because the Prince had indicated an interest in this traveller. He struggled to hide his resentment of this girl behind a polite facade.

Tenuli discovered in herself a reserve of confidence and bravado she had not suspected was there, answering Korak's question in a steady, clear voice.

Eluron contributed little to the interview, but silently watched this stranger as she gradually manipulated the conversation to her advantage. Something in her manner — her voice, perhaps — seemed to paint in his mind a place both strange and familiar, a land of greater light and joy than any he had found since he had stumbled into Hindalom and Milo at the edge of the Grey City.

And this curious effect made Eluron decide to speak with this young lady alone, as soon as the opportunity presented itself.

THIRTEEN

As a result of the interview with Korak, Tenuli was offered, and accepted, the position of Head of Domestic Arrangements for the Scarlet Castle. The instructions to take her on in this position had come from the Prince himself, though Tenuli had not yet seen him. All things seemed to be relayed through Korak. From time to time she wondered whether and where she might see the Prince, but most of her energies went into becoming familiar with the castle routine so that she could *appear* to be doing her job well.

For that was the key to the success of her plan. She intended to gain the confidence of Korak first, and then hopefully the Prince as well, so that she could discover the detailed lay-out of the castle. This information she would then smuggle back to Toth, thus causing him to admire her courage and cunning, and to realize that she was much more than an innocent little girl who couldn't follow him into danger. What Toth might do with this information she cared little, though she assumed he would pass it on to the Knight of Roses. Her motive was entirely self-centered, namely her desire to have Toth all to herself. She was not doing it for truth or goodness; she was not moved by any desire to restore the light of a higher realm to the Shadowland: her wish was to attain her own personal happiness, with no thought of helping anyone else.

But there were other plans afoot too, which Tenuli was not aware of. Firstly there was the Prince's plot to tempt her into the darkness of his influence, by appealing to her selfish desire to have Toth all to herself. It must be understood that the Prince was able to tune in to the thoughts of all those whose motives were selfish, mean or cruel, because it was from those very thoughts that he derived his strength. In fact, the Prince had known of Tenuli's state of mind from the very moment she had given in to jealousy during the ride with Toth away from Sandria, and he had been aware of her plan and progress ever since. He also knew the thoughts of Sindor, because of the latter's resentful, violent streak. That was the flaw that allowed the Prince to link with Sindor's mind.

By contrast, the evil master of the Scarlet Castle could never perceive the thoughts of Toth or the Silent One. Both of these men were fully devoted to the Knight of Roses, and were committed to restoring the light of Moralia to the Shadowland. They were entirely innocent of selfish motive, and neither greed nor cruelty were in their make-up. This purity was like a shield around them, through which the Prince's probing could never penetrate.

But then there was the Greater Plan: the carefully arranged pattern that was orchestrated by Jelander from his location in Moralia. This was a special plan for Tenuli's development and self-realization, and took into account both the lesser selfish plot to win Toth's heart, and the counter-plot of the Prince. Jelander had fully expected Tenuli to react as she did to Toth's refusal to commit a personal love to her, and had known without a doubt that the Prince of Shades would undertake to tempt her away from her instinctive goodness. For that was the role of the Prince: to test the insight and purity of Moralians who came within his influence. Though Toth believed that the evil master of the Scarlet Castle wished to destroy all those who dwelt in the Shadowland, this assessment was not entirely accurate. The Prince's main motive was to drag Moralians down to the same base level that Korak had reached, from which there was no hope of return to the light and joy of the higher realms. And for many individuals — ones like Hindalom, Milo and Eluron — this could more effectively be done by involving them in the Prince's work.

But the Prince of Shades was not aware of Jelander's plan or influence, though he knew generally of the existence of Moralia and the effects of the Pathways of Change. Jelander's pure unselfish light was vastly higher than the rough, coarse vibration of the evil Prince, which meant that the wise teacher knew all about the plans of the Prince, while the latter knew nothing at all of Jelander.

And Jelander knew something else that the Prince was

unaware of: that Doran — whose affection for Tenuli was untainted by any selfish motive — was soon to be projected into the subterranean passages beneath the Scarlet Castle itself. And because of that purity, neither the Prince, Korak nor any of the others would know that he had come.

FOURTEEN

Toth was not overly surprised when he returned to the cabins and learned that Tenuli had galloped off toward the Scarlet Castle, for the Silent One had indicated to him the night before that she would likely attempt something of the sort. He was happy to learn that the Silent One had given her a pouch of fresh well water, for he knew that it would serve her both as a weapon and as a reminder of the truth.

"All things happen according to a larger plan," he said, "in time we shall see where these events lead."

They decided not to give chase since she had clearly chosen to go in this way. Early the next day, Toth, Sindor and the Silent One set off for the stronghold of the Knight of Roses on the three remaining animals, leaving Fromil and Blenik in the small cabins. They had agreed that within two days one of them would return with extra horses.

Far to the west, in the giant Redwood Forest, lay the stronghold of the Knight of Roses. As Toth approached the forest, he noted again the feeling of lightness and optimism which floated in the air of this place. The sky was still a seamless grey layer of dullness as it was everywhere in the Shadowland, but if ever there was a spark of something brighter than shadows and grander than selfishness and cruelty, it was here.

From high in the trees a bird-song sounded. Toth recognized it as a signal from the Knight's advance look-out that he and the others had come. The bird call was almost but not quite accurate, and it seemed to echo off ahead of them as the news of their arrival was picked up and passed by other look-outs spaced at intervals along the path. This signalling system had warned the Knight many times of the approach of scouting parties from the Prince of Shades, without the intruders realizing that their presence had been noted.

Toth and the other two continued into the forest toward the heart of the stronghold. From time to time they heard a special bird call above them, and recognized it as a salutation of welcome from another follower of the Knight of Roses. Toth had also learned to communicate by these whistled messages, and occasionally returned the calls when they came.

They were entering an area where the giant trees rose hundreds of feet into the air. Numerous whistled calls proceeded from the branches above their heads as they pulled their mounts to a halt under a gigantic redwood whose trunk measured more than twenty feet in diameter. A rope ladder snaked down before them. Toth grasped it and held it steady as Sindor began to climb. The Silent One was next and Toth followed third.

From a height of eighty feet up to about two hundred feet, the leafy canopy of some thirty trees had been transformed by the Knight's men into an intricate beehive of activity, with large, sheltered platforms cantilevered out from the larger trunks at several levels, catwalks of vine and rope slung delicately between them, strong knotted cords hanging down to allow single men to swing from one station to another, and in one tree an entire two-level enclosed structure built of boards and thatch with windows and doors.

It was toward this treetop building, gently swaying on its lofty perch some hundred and fifty feet above the grassy carpet beneath, that Toth and his two companions climbed. As they rose through the various levels, they called greetings to many of the men working nearby on the platforms and passageways. Some were preparing food over a small fire, others were cleaning a number of individual water pouches to be filled from the large bag which the Silent One had brought on his horse, and still others were repairing saddles, boots and other equipment needed by the Knight's men.

Inside the main building, the Knight of Roses sensed the vibration caused whenever the rope ladder was in use. He arose from the maps over which he had been poring, walked to the door, and opened it. Smiling as he recognized his guests, he reached down to help each of them through the doorway and into the small room.

The Knight was a tall, well-proportioned man, with dark eyes that were wide-set and trusting. This, combined with a ready smile and his willingness to do anything for the comfort and convenience of others, made him seem at first glance rather unlike a leader of men. But upon digging deeper into this complex personality, one came quickly upon a hard bedrock of purpose and determination — that gritty courage that could inspire the timid with resolve, and the apathetic with a passionate loyalty.

Early in his present sojourn, the Knight — like so many others who had also come in along the Fifth Pathway of Change — had tended to assume the best of a person until the worst were demonstrated, always giving the benefit of the doubt, always ready to ignore faults and imperfections. Indeed, his blithe supposition that all men were as guileless and honest as he had more than once led him into decisions he later regretted. And yet through this process he was seeking a balance — a middle path between two opposing tendencies: for in earlier sojourns in the Shadowland the Knight had been altogether too suspicious and mistrustful of others, too given to assuming dark motives even when none were present. This in turn had led him to be secretive and hidden, and had prompted him to practice manipulating others. These were typical Eighth Pathway traits, but had often surfaced in him even when the Eighth had not been the route of entry. His teachers hoped that now, with the impress of the Fifth Pathway heavy upon him, the Knight would learn to blend these opposing exaggerations together into a balanced counterpoint, ending at last with a healthy ability to applaud and support the positive traits of others, while remaining unblinded to their flaws. Toward this noble goal the Knight of Roses had come far.

The last of his guests had now entered. Turning, he hugged each of the travellers in welcome. Then he flashed a white smile and said to Toth, "well, my friend, what news do you bring? I see by the full water bag on the horse below that your mission to the Well of Tears was successful. Yet your wound suggests the attempt to fill it went not unchallenged."

"We encountered two guards sent by the Prince to keep travellers from the well," answered Toth. "I tricked one of them into looking down into the water. He remembered the truth and subsequently joined us. The other attacked me and had to be subdued by the Silent One. We left him tied by the well." Toth then recounted their meeting with Tenuli and her subsequent escape toward the castle on one of the horses. The Knight raised an eyebrow at this story, but was naturally more interested in the details of the Prince's activities.

"So he *has* begun his campaign against the Well of Tears," mused the Knight as he turned and walked over to the maps spread out on the table. "We shall have to take action sooner than I thought."

Sindor gestured impatiently. "Let them begin," he said, "I for one am ready."

The Knight raised his eyes and regarded Sindor. "I see," he said slowly, "that you are as ready as ever to break heads in the cause of truth."

Sindor looked at the Knight, then down to the ground. "They tortured my friend..." he began in a low voice. "It is right to be revenged upon them."

The Knight came and put his arm around Sindor's shoulder. "My friend," he said, "so long as you harbour vengeance within you the evil Prince of Shades can tap your mind, because thoughts of revenge and a desire to get even are of the same quality as the Prince himself. Even now he is aware of what we are saying in this room, because your lust for vengeance makes you an unwitting spy in our

56

midst. If you cannot overcome this craving for revenge, you will have to wait on the nearby platform. It would not do for the Prince of Shades to learn our plans."

"It is so hard for me," replied Sindor as tears began to form in his eyes.

"Remember that they are our brothers, Sindor. In a higher realm we knew them all as friends. Only Korak and a few of the cruellest henchmen of the Prince are to be shunned, for they have sunk so far into evil that even the water from the Well of Tears cannot redeem them. But the others have merely forgotten what you are fortunate to remember. We need you to help us in the task that looms ahead, but you must learn to wish them well, not ill. Victory for us does not mean destroying the Prince's army, but rather winning them over to the light of truth."

"I will try my best," replied Sindor. Toth hugged him and the Silent One put a gentle hand on his shoulder. The Knight opened the door and Sindor went out.

FIFTEEN

The Knight of Roses then proceeded to outline his plan for counteracting the Prince's campaign to close the Well of Tears.

"We have word from our scouts in the Grey City that the Prince will first send a bunch of the Stalkers like Hindalom to Sandria, probably to intimidate and harass travellers. We think it likely that he will then dispatch a small group from his private castle guard to do the actual work of breaking down the wall and filling in the well. They are known to be loyal to the Prince, and most of them are almost lost to the evil influence of that place. However the Prince must make his selection carefully. He must choose men who are loyal enough to be counted on to follow orders, especially the order not to drink from or look into the well. But at the same time the men must not be so evil that merely being close to the well causes them pain.

"Now I believe that any man who can approach the Well

of Tears without discomfort has enough decency and light remaining in him to be able to remember the truth upon looking into or drinking the water. All we have to do is to find some way to bring them into contact with it. Probably our best chance is to use the pouches and try to dash water directly in their faces.

"Our first goal is to have our own men in control of the well. Then we move to phase two. We use heated rocks to turn some of the well water into *steam* so that it will drift as vapour in the air to the region immediately surrounding the well. We have found out that breathing the well water in as vapour has about the same effect as drinking it, so long as enough of the steam is taken in. This will give us a protective screen around the well. Anyone who attacks will either remember the truth and join us, or retreat because of the pain that the vapour causes him.

"So here's how it will be done. As soon as we're in control of the well, we carry in several large rocks that have been pre-heated in a fire at the edge of town. Some of us will stay there, gradually pouring water on the rocks to set up the vapour shield. Then the rest will start phase three.

"Now we fully expect the Prince to have assembled most of his army just a few miles out of Sandria — far enough away for Korak and the other really evil ones to remain without great pain. Some of the reports we have received indicate that part of his army is already mobilizing and will soon be underway. The Prince will want to have these troops at the ready, in case we are able to frustrate his initial attempt to close the well. When he learns that we have done so, he will probably give the order to attack Sandria *en masse*, with some of his cavalry carrying stones to throw into the well.

"However we must act *before* he gives that order. Our plan is to time our first raid just as the army is preparing for nighttime in their encampment. They will light a number of large fires for cooking and heat, and most of the men will be close to those fires.

"The moment we have taken over the well, a crew headed by the Silent One will begin to pull up water, filling five large bags like the one you brought with you today. These will be strapped to our strongest horses, and then five riders will mount up and head at top speed for the army encampment. This must be timed to be late enough for the fires to be burning, but early enough for there to be sufficient light to see the way. That means our initial raid must take place about an hour before dusk.

"The riders will have their daggers in hand. Each will follow a path which curves around the edge of one of the army fires. As he passes the fire he will slash the bag open, spilling the water directly on the flames. All of the soldiers who breathe in the resulting steam and vapour will be affected.

"The rest of our own men will wait in the forest just outside the camp until they see our five riders dash up. As soon as they hear the hiss of water as it hits the fires, they will move in. They will have to be prepared for anything — from explaining things for someone who has been confused, to defending themselves from attack by the really evil ones. But the water vapour in the air should swing the struggle in our favour.

"We have no way of knowing whether the Prince will be in the encampment. He is rarely seen except by his closest aides such as Korak. However if he *is* in the camp we shall try our best to dowse him with well water. Based on the pain which the water causes to any who are really evil, I believe that soaking the Prince will mean the end of him. And the end of the Prince will mean the first ray of true light for the Shadowland."

SIXTEEN

The musty smell of damp rocks had long ago invaded every cranny of the torch-lit dungeons under the Scarlet Castle, and upon that unsavory odor floated here and there a whiff of stale blood mixed with human excrement. Along one of the corridors a number of cells had been hewn out of the granite rock, and six of these were occupied by an assortment of cadaverous prisoners who sat dejectedly on the rough floor, their tortured bodies barely clinging to a flicker of the life-force that once had enlivened them.

Three jailers stood together at one end of the corridor trading gossip about castle events, while near them two evil-looking dogs growled menace at each other over the boney remains of some dead animal which had been sent down from the kitchen. Over this dismal scene hovered an aura of hopelessness and fear so thick that it clung to one's skin like a clammy poultice of despair.

And into that dreadful place of pain and horror, with the memory of Moralia still fresh in his mind, Doran was projected. He came in along the Third Pathway of Change, which gives one an added cleverness not normally a part of the Moralian existence. Jelander had suggested that Doran take on the Third Pathway, hopeful that an experience in which the mind was quickened beyond its normal limits would cause Doran to seek an *understanding* of himself that he did not normally search for when in the lower world.

"Shadowland," Jelander had explained to him, "is like a special hall of mirrors, which shows us aspects of ourselves that we might not normally perceive while in Moralia. Or you could think of it in terms of a chemical experiment: your own being is an unknown fluid that you wish to analyze, in order to determine what chemicals are dissolved in it. The Shadowland gives you a series of test-liquids that you can add in, and the observed colour changes tell you what the constituents are. But you must *understand* how to do the analysis, and the Third Pathway of Change enhances your mental grasp of things so that you can reason your way through it."

But right now Doran did not feel too clear in his mind. He took a breath of the stale, foul air, then suppressed a cough as his lungs contracted in protest against the putrid smell.

Not far away, Doran heard the growling and snapping of the dogs, and a shudder went through him as he wondered

60

whether they were tearing to shreds the body of some hapless torture victim.

Blinking to accustom himself to the dimness, he took stock of where he was. Jelander had told him that he would have to be projected directly into one of the empty but unlocked cells, so that none of the jailers would see his appearance. That seemed to be what had happened. Doran's back was against a cold, rocky surface. A rough doorway was to his left, and through it a wall torch sent its fitful shafts of pale, flickering light to fall against the rough stone wall facing him. But Doran himself was in shadow, so that anyone who chanced along the corridor would not be able to glance in and see him.

And luckily so, for no sooner had he found his bearings than a footfall sounded just outside the door. Then a shadow was outlined on the wall he was facing.

"Send the big dog down here," shouted the coarse voice of the jailer. "We can lock him in this empty cell until the other one has had his food. Killer! In here, you bloody brute!"

Doran heard the dog's paws on the rocky floor of the corridor, and his heart leaped to his throat. The jailer meant to lock the beast in with him! He shrank back further into the shadows.

The iron gate of the cell creaked on its hinges as the jailer moved it into a position from where he could quickly slam it shut. Doran saw by the shadow on the opposite wall that the man had a stick and was poking it out in front of him. A deep, rolling growl came from the dog's throat. Suddenly it lunged at the jailer! Crack! The stick struck a glancing blow to the side of the dog's head. Then they closed together, the dog straining to reach the jailer's throat with his powerful jaws, the jailer fending him off with his hands. They collapsed in a heap of fury on the ground, half in and half out of Doran's cell. The footsteps of the other jailers sounded in the distance as they ran toward where the two were locked in combat.

Doran had been terrified up to this point, but now his mind cleared. Suddenly he saw what to do in order to turn this desperate situation around. Quickly he stepped forward out of the shadows, bent over and grabbed the jailer's coat near the collar. The huge dog was so intent upon destroying the jailer that he did not notice as Doran dragged both of them further into the dank cell, leaving them struggling in the fitful light of the wall torch. Then he stepped back again into the shadows.

The other two men ran into the cell. One of them had a length of chain which he looped around the dog's neck and yanked. The other bent to help the jailer on the ground. Neither of them noticed Doran waiting in the shadows.

The dog yelped loudly as the chain tightened around his neck. Doran saw that both of the jailers who had just arrived had their backs to him. 'Now or never,' he thought. Quickly he stepped through the doorway of the cell, and moved off down the corridor away from the direction that the jailers had come from. The sound of shouting and struggle faded behind him as he ran.

At the end of the corridor he came to a flight of wooden stairs, leading up to a trap door which was now closed. 'And not locked, I hope,' thought Doran as he quickly climbed the steps. He pushed on the trap door...and it swung upwardly under his pressure! In a trice he was through the door and had it closed behind him.

'Now to find Tenuli,' he thought to himself. 'I wonder where she can be in this dismal place.'

*   *   *

In Moralia, Jelander nodded to himself. "The Third Pathway of Change," he mused. "Without that extra mind boost Doran might never have seen his way out of the predicament into which he was projected. It is good that he agreed to be tested in this way. Already I can perceive a brighter colour in his mental quality. But we shall see whether his understanding of himself is improved by this effect."

SEVENTEEN

For days Tenuli had busied herself learning the household routine of the castle, but now she judged that it was time to carry out her real plan, which was to discover the basic lay-out of the building. How she would communicate this intelligence to Toth she did not know, but she would deal with that problem after she had made her investigations.

She had noticed an increase in activity within the castle over the last forty-eight hours, with numerous rough-looking men coming and going and many meetings behind closed doors. It concerned her that with so many extra people in the castle her chances of being caught snooping around were greater. However she decided that this increase in activity signalled a possible attack on Toth's group, and she concluded that she must act without delay regardless of the heightened danger.

Her motive was still mainly selfish — her desire to win Toth's admiration and eventually his love — but she had seen enough of the Prince's followers to know that they were a nasty lot, and the still, small voice of truth in her heart told her clearly that she must soon get away from the evil Scarlet Castle.

The man who had taken her to the first meeting with Korak, Eluron, was also on her mind much of the time. She sensed that Eluron was not committed to darkness in the same way as Korak or some of the others, and it occurred to her that perhaps if she talked to him about the things she had already found out, he could be persuaded to escape with her when the time came for her to flee. She was not so blithely optimistic as to think that her snooping would never be noticed, especially by Korak, whose eagle eyes seemed to flicker constantly from thing to thing and from person to person, as he took in everything around him.

In fact, Korak caused her a great deal of uncertainty at all times. She had realized even in their first meeting that this rough, evil man was only feigning cordiality, and that any kind of pleasantness was totally foreign to his nature.

She knew that Korak resented her, and had been somehow forced to treat her civilly. The sooner she could put a healthy distance between them, the happier she would be.

Tenuli began her investigations in the Great Hall, under the long, hanging tapestries with their scenes of silent massacre, their noiseless battles bathed in blood. She had already gotten a clear picture in her head of the arrangement of rooms and corridors on the second floor level where her own bedroom was located, because the storerooms, pantries, kitchens and linen-closets were also on that same level, and her duties revolved around those areas. But she knew there were meeting rooms and studies on the first floor, and she felt intuitively that Toth would need to know most about the lower level since that is where any invading force would first enter the Scarlet Castle.

Tenuli surveyed the enormous room in which she was now standing. Along an end wall she noticed a series of oaken panels about two feet square, and she was drawn to them because none of the other walls was decorated in the same way. The tops of the panels were just above her head, but she judged that she could probably feel along the tops with her hand even though she might not see fully what was there.

She walked to the end panel and began to examine its edges, looking for...she wasn't sure what. Maybe one of them was false and could be pushed aside. Perhaps a key was hidden along a border. Perhaps...

Suddenly Tenuli froze. Footsteps were coming toward the Great Hall along the corridor that led in from the main gate — the same entrance that she had been brought through on the first night. She looked around for something that she could appear to be attending to legitimately. After all, she *was* part of the castle staff. In the corner was a small desk with drawers, and a padded chair behind it. Quickly she went to it, sat down and pulled out the top drawer. Thank goodness! The drawer contained a sheaf of paper and several pencils. Tenuli pulled out a sheet and pretended to be writing something.

"What the devil are you doing in the Great Hall?" came

Korak's harsh voice, resounding like a whip-crack through the enormous room. He stood at the far end, his large shoulders framed in the doorway.

"Uh, it was hot in my room," she replied, looking at him bravely in the face. "I had to make some lists of needed supplies, so I came down here hoping it would be cooler."

Korak regarded her in silence for a moment, then strode over to the desk and glowered down at her.

"There are many places in the Scarlet Castle where no members of the domestic staff are allowed to go," he growled. "The Great Hall is one of them. The Prince wishes to preserve the memory of his victories away from the prying eyes of those who do not deserve to experience his greatness. Return to your room, and do not let me catch you in this hall again."

Tenuli looked at him boldly. "When I first came here I was brought in through the Great Hall," she said.

Korak's face twisted in anger, "They should have taken you in through the side entrance. Only warriors come in this way. Now get out of here!"

Somewhere she found the audacity to say, "not until I finish this list. It is too hot in my room to work."

The evil face in front of her blackened even more. "Do not test me," Korak hissed, "or you will regret ever having set eyes on the Scarlet Castle." With that he turned and strode off toward the main corridor.

Tenuli tried to suppress the shaking in her body. Never before had she been confronted with such an evil presence; never before had so much venom and hatred been directed at her. She waited until she could no longer hear his retreating footsteps, and then she got up and resumed her investigation of the panels, surprising herself that she had the courage to defy Korak.

Along the top edge of the fourth panel from the side wall, Tenuli's hand touched something cold and solid. 'A switch or a knob,' she thought to herself. Gingerly she began to push and pull on the metal protrusion between her fingers, and suddenly it slid to the left about half an inch. The moment this happened, the panel itself fell ajar, opening out a few inches like a small door hinged at one side. From behind the panel came a gentle drumming sound, like several baby-rattles all being shaken together. Curious, she pulled it full open and peered inside to see what was there. A small passageway the same size as the panel led down at a slight angle but the light in the Great Hall was not good enough for her to see very far along it. Carefully she reached in through the opening, feeling along with her fingers. The bottom was cold and metallic. She stretched in further...further...and then her fingers closed on something soft and scaly.

With a cry of fright she pulled back her hand as the first rattlesnake shoved its head through the open panel door. Then two more appeared as the first one flopped down on the floor and began slithering toward her. Suppressing a scream of terror, Tenuli ran straight for the side hall which led to the stairs. She rushed up them two at a time, and then on the upper level she slowed to a brisk walk, hoping no one had noticed her hasty arrival. Inside her bedroom she bolted the door from the inside, then collapsed on the bed, shaking uncontrollably.

* * *

In Moralia, Jelander had watched the scene with interest. "She has much courage, Trillamar," he said. "But she will need even more soon, for the only way she will be able to escape from the Scarlet Castle will be to go through that same snake passage."

EIGHTEEN

Doran glanced behind him as he heard footsteps approaching along the corridor. He stepped into the shadow of a darkened doorway as two castle guards turned the corner and headed his way.

"But how did the snakes get out?" asked one of the guards.

"Damned if I know. Korak just said put them back inside

the chamber." The guards passed the doorway without looking to the side.

"One thing I can't stand, it's snakes," said the first guard as they disappeared around another corner. Doran let out the breath he had been holding. Then he moved off in the direction from which the guards had come. Shortly he came to a flight of stairs leading upwards. He stood uncertainly for a moment, then began climbing the steps to the second floor.

At the top, he could hear a bustle of noise off to the left, and from the smells he judged that the kitchens must lie in that direction. In front of him were a row of cupboard doors, one of which was open. Through it he could see shelves with what appeared to be sheets or linen of some kind. On a hunch he went to the doors and opened them one by one. In the third cupboard he found what he was looking for: several white outfits of the kind worn by kitchen helpers. Taking one that appeared about the right size, Doran headed along the passageway toward the kitchen. No one had yet seen him.

He shortly came to a partly open door, through which he could see an empty room. Quickly he ducked inside and put on the white clothing. Then he took a deep breath and stepped back into the passageway.

Just at that moment two other kitchen workers passed the doorway, heading toward the kitchen.

"Hey!" exclaimed one of them. "Who are you? Haven't seen you before."

Doran tried to act casual. "Supposed to help out in the kitchen," he began.

"Must be new help because there are more guests in the castle," said the other worker. "What's your name?"

"Doran."

"Alright. You better come with us. Were you in the guards before?"

"Uh, yes — in the guards."

He followed the other two into a pantry and began to help them take inventory of the supplies.

In her bedroom, Tenuli had overcome her shaking and now lay quietly, trying to decide what to do next. She knew that the snakes would soon be discovered, and she assumed that the news would be delivered to Korak, who would immediately conclude that she had let them out while snooping around after he had left the Great Hall.

She glanced over at the dresser top, and noticed the small water-pouch. 'Oh yes,' she thought. 'The pouch that the Silent One gave me.' Feeling slightly thirsty, she got up and went over to the dresser. She picked up the pouch, pulled out the small stopper, and raised the nozzle opening to her lips.

Now it must be realized that Tenuli did not remember that the water had the ability to make her recall her purpose in coming to the Shadowland. In fact, she had already completely forgotten Moralia, Jelander, the Great River — everything. Thus she did not realize that drinking the water would completely change her perspective on her existence in the lower world. Right now her only desire was to escape from the Scarlet Castle and find some way to rejoin Toth, since the events of the past half-hour had convinced her that it would not be possible to complete her investigation of the castle's lay-out. But if her lips touched the water in that pouch...

Bang! Bang! came two sharp blows on the door. "Open up!" said a man's voice. "You are to be taken to Korak!"

She lowered the pouch without drinking, and shrank back against the wall.

"Open up!" The voice was louder this time. Then the knob turned as the guard tried to force the door.

"The bolt's thrown from the inside," said another voice. "She's got to be in there. Let's break the door down."

A second passed.

Whump! The sound of burly shoulders hitting the door made Tenuli start.

Whump! Another blow, and the door began to splinter. WHUMP! The door flew open and in stumbled the two guards.

"There she is!" shouted the taller one as he caught his

balance.

"Grab her!" The other guard lunged forward as Tenuli side-stepped. Desperately her mind raced to find some way out of this lethal predicament. She knew that if she fell into Korak's power it would be the end of her. Obviously he had found out about the snake episode, and intended to punish her for disobeying him.

She looked down at her hands, still holding the uncorked pouch. 'Water!' she thought. 'Maybe I can squirt enough in their eyes to stop them for a moment while I run out the door.' Quickly she raised the pouch, aimed, and squeezed a jet of water in both guards' faces.

What happened next took her completely by surprise. The smaller guard reeled back as if a pile-driver had hit him in the chest. The taller guard put his hands to his face. "Aaaieee – " he screamed. "My eyes! They're on fire! It must be acid!" He crumpled up on the floor groaning in pain and trying to wipe the liquid away from his face.

The smaller guard had sat down in confusion. "What is this place–?" He was too disoriented to pay any attention to Tenuli as she slipped out the doorway and into the corridor.

She walked quickly toward the kitchen area, hoping to lose herself among the staff there. 'The pantries have many cupboards and storage bins,' she thought to herself. 'I can always duck out of sight if more guards come.' She had no definite plan, aside from hanging tight to the water pouch that had somehow incapacitated both guards and allowed her to escape.

Entering the main larder, she tried to appear as casual as possible. Off to the side in the first pantry she saw one of the kitchen helpers taking inventory. He had his back to her and she did not recognize him.

Suddenly there was a commotion at the far end of the cookery in front of her. "Haven't seen her here today," came the cook's high-pitched voice.

"She's dangerous," replied the guard. "If you see her, report to security at once!" Tenuli saw the heads of three guards in the distance, coming her way and looking from

69

side to side.

Quickly she stepped over to the pantry where the worker was taking inventory. "You there," she tried to sound like the confident Head of Domestic Arrangements. "Come with me to the far end of the pantry." She brushed past him without looking at his face, and led the way to a row of large bulk-food bins at the back of the narrow, shelved room.

As she walked, her mind raced to find some way of hiding herself while ensuring that this man would not give her away. Seconds later she reached the large bins, without anything having occurred to her. 'It's no use,' she thought. She turned around and her shoulders sagged.

"Help me," she pleaded as she raised her eyes to the tall man's face. "The guards are looking—" She caught her breath.

Doran was smiling at her. "Tenuli," he said gently, "my sweet Tenuli."

She looked into the eyes she had loved in Moralia, and a memory flickered. "Who are you?" she asked in surprise.

"A friend," he chuckled. "But I fear we've no time for reminiscing. Are those guards looking for you?" She nodded in reply. "Then climb into this empty bin," he said, lifting the lid and offering his hand. "I will keep them away."

Tenuli felt bewildered and yet peaceful and safe at the same time, as if a long voyage through troubled waters had ended. Somehow this tall, gentle man — this dear stranger — would find a way to rescue her from the terror of the Scarlet Castle. She knew it in her heart.

Then suddenly she remembered the water-pouch. "Here," she said, handing it to him. "I think it has acid or something in it. You may have to use it on the guards."

Doran took the pouch from her, shoved it into a pocket, then closed the lid of the bin and pretended to be counting containers along a nearby shelf.

"Hey you in there!" The guard's voice was rough-edged. "You alone?"

"Yes." Doran turned and walked toward the guard.

70

"There were two other workers but they left to check some of the other pantries."

"Humph," grunted the guard. "We're looking for the woman Tenuli. If you see her, let one of the guards know."

"Sure," said Doran. The guard disappeared from the entranceway.

Curious about the pouch Tenuli had given him, Doran took it from his pocket as he walked back toward the bin where she was hiding. He lifted the lid and helped Tenuli to her feet. "Danger's past," he said, smiling. Then he unstopped the pouch nozzle and sniffed the contents. "Smells like plain water to me," he remarked. "Are you sure it's acid?"

"I don't know what it is, but it burned the eyes of one of the two guards that Korak sent to take me from my room."

"And the other guard?"

"He just seemed to be stunned by it."

Doran dropped some of the pouch water on his finger and touched it to his tongue.

The effect on Doran of contacting the water from the Well of Tears was not as dramatic as it might have been for a typical Moralian in the Shadowland. For one thing, he had only just arrived. For another, he had been allowed to retain a relatively clear picture of his life in Moralia, thanks to certain mental exercises which Jelander had taught to him just before he had entered along the Third Pathway of Change. That is why he recognized Tenuli when he first saw her in the pantry, and why he could remember her name.

You see, Doran's primary mission during this particular sojourn in the Shadowland was to stand ready to rescue or help Tenuli if and when she got herself into a sticky position. And that was another reason for sending him in along the Third Pathway — the one that lends an increased clarity and quickness to the mind. Because of this special mission, it was necessary for him to avoid the loss of

71

memory that the Shadowland usually caused.

Thus, as Doran tasted the water in the pouch, he simply experienced a greater acuity of memory than he already had in terms of Moralia, his teacher Jelander, and his mission in the Shadowland. In addition, a pleasant glow suffused itself through his heart as the water spread its effect. And suddenly Doran knew what the water was. He remembered about the Well of Tears, and he became certain that the pouch had been filled from its water.

Doran realized that if he and Tenuli were to have the best chance for escape from this dangerous place, she too would have to remember Moralia, and particularly to remember *him* — so that she would trust him.

"Here," he said, handing the pouch toward her. "It is water from the Well of Tears. It will let you remember who I am, and where we both have come from."

Dubiously she raised the pouch and smelled the opening. Then she put the nozzle to her lips and drank a small sip.

The effect on Tenuli was like a rush of remembered joy, a flooding in of truth and purpose that had slipped away from her conscious recall. She turned and gazed with love on her dear friend from the land beyond the last colour of the last rainbow.

"Doran!" she said. "Doran!" Half laughing, half crying, Tenuli embraced him. He put his strong arms around her and held her close.

"Little friend," he whispered. "Time enough to remember it all. But now we must act quickly. The guards are scouring this place for you, and it's only a matter of time before they decide to look in every closet, bin and secret compartment of the castle. How do we get out of here?"

"There's one main entrance and several side gates. Also a secret passage somewhere that tunnels under the rock and opens through the terrain behind the castle. But I haven't found out how to get into it."

"Where will they *expect* you to try to escape?"

"Probably at the side gates. The regular staff is not allowed to use the main entrance because the approach is through the main hall, and that is off-limits except for the Prince's warriors."

"Then that is precisely how we shall leave this dismal, forsaken place."

Tenuli looked slyly at Doran. "Before we do," she said with a wink, "let's leave the castle staff a small going-away present. I think a certain special ingredient should be added to the big soup pot that everyone is served from." She held up the pouch. "If that small taste of well water was all that was necessary for me, then even if we dilute it in the soup, it should bring back a lot of memories for a lot of people."

Doran grinned at her. "But let's save a little in the pouch," he said. "We may need to defend ourselves from the castle guard. Here, let me do the addition, since everyone is on the look-out for you. Wait here, I'll be back as soon as I can."

Taking the pouch from Tenuli, Doran slipped out into the corridor. He headed for the main kitchen, where he could see the huge iron soup-pot already steaming over the wood fire beneath. Pretending to be counting supplies in the cabinets close by the pot, he waited until a worker who was stirring the pot paused to chat with one of the other helpers that happened by.

Doran walked to the side opposite to where the two were chatting. Neither worker was watching the pot. Quickly he unstopped the pouch. Then, holding it close to the outside of the pot and below the top rim, he squeezed it and squirted a jet of well water in a curving trajectory up and over the rim. He heard the water splashing into the soup, and when he judged that about half the contents of the pouch had been expelled, he replaced the stopper, slipped the pouch into a pocket, and headed back to the pantry where he had left Tenuli.

In the pantry Tenuli waited nervously. Several minutes had passed. Where was Doran?

Then she heard approaching footsteps. 'Thank goodness,' she thought. A tall silhouette framed itself in the doorway.

73

"Doran!" she cried.

"No!" said Korak, laughing evilly as he moved toward her. "But if he is a friend of yours, he will soon be in chains, along with you!"

NINETEEN

Eluron's chambers were on the third floor of the east wing, very close to the counting room where the Prince's wealth was kept. His duties included keeping track of the stacks of gold and silver bars, and he visited the room more often than his work required, so that he could gratify his avarice by running his fingers over the shiny metal. His own chambers were sumptuously appointed, and this too gave him much pleasure. In addition, the Prince was paying him handsomely for his services.

But during the past week, ever since he had accompanied the young woman to her meeting with Korak, Eluron had been brooding and absent-minded. There had been something special about her — an air of purity, perhaps — that seemed to remind him of a place once familiar but now forgotten, a land as innocent, as good, as Tenuli herself.

For two days now he had been going over the records of the castle, trying to understand the half-scrawled ledger-entries of his predecessor. But his mind was preoccupied, and he found it hard to concentrate. From time to time Korak called him down to discuss some point to do with castle finances, and the more Eluron saw of him, the less he liked him. Only this morning he had been in the war-room with Korak when they were interrupted by a jailer from the dungeons beneath the castle.

"Well?" Korak looked up at the jailer, annoyed at the intrusion.

"It's killer," the man answered. "Trad was attacked by the brute when he tried to lock it in one of the empty cells. We had to, uh, subdue the dog."

"What do you mean subdue?" growled Korak, rising from his chair. "Killer is a good tracking dog."

"Well, I used a chain around his neck to pull him off Trad,

and I think his wind-pipe must have collapsed—"

"What?" shouted Korak. "Is he alive or dead?"

"Dead," said the guard, backing away.

"Then within two hours you will wish you were the same," said Korak slowly. "Guards! Take this man to the Chamber of Cooperation. He is in need of a 'treatment' on one of our special machines." Korak laughed wickedly as his personal guards dragged the man away.

That was the first Eluron had heard about the Chamber of Cooperation, and the phrase sent a chill down his spine. He could imagine what dreadful devices might be used to enforce 'cooperation'...

It was with a sense of relief that Eluron climbed back to his chambers. After the incident with the jailer, he had been unable to concentrate on the discussion, and he could sense Korak's irritation with his vague answers.

Eluron felt he needed some fresh air, and decided to take a walk outside the castle. He did not wish to be seen, so he made his way through a little-used doorway on the east side, then walked around to the bushy terrain behind the castle.

The outside air felt good to him after the musty atmosphere of the castle. Eluron found a footpath among the bushes and aimlessly wandered along it, lost in his own thoughts. 'There is danger here,' he said to himself. 'Korak is thoroughly evil and would happily destroy anyone who crossed him. Why did I ever agree to work in the castle in the first place?'

He noticed that the path was becoming fainter and he stopped to determine whether he had somehow gotten off on the wrong track. He looked to his left and saw what appeared to be a cleared footpath about twenty feet away. Turning, he walked through the brush, wiping the branches away from his face. But when he reached the position he had thought was a cleared path, it turned out to be just a boggy, damp area too wet to allow bushes to grow.

Again he turned, now a little concerned that he might not locate the path he had come on. Suddenly he heard a voice from somewhere close by.

"Careful with that water bag. If you spill any of it, Korak will have your head off."

Eluron ducked out of sight behind a low bush.

"What's so special about water?" came another voice.

"Korak says it's poison-water from the Well of Tears, and he wants us to find a way to neutralize its effect. Says it burns some people but not others."

"So why the secrecy?"

"Korak says he doesn't want any of the regular staff to drink the water by mistake. No one is supposed to know it's in the castle laboratory."

Eluron saw the two men come into view along the path he had originally been following. Neither of them could see where Eluron was hiding.

"Where's this tunnel then?" asked the second man, staggering a little under the heavy weight of the water bag.

"It's supposed to be close to here," replied the first man. "Instructions are to find a large rock with a white spot on one side, then walk directly away from the spotted side about thirty paces. There should be a disguised trap-door at that location."

The men moved further along the path, and their voices became muffled. Eluron waited another ten minutes, then rose from his crouched position.

'A tunnel?' he thought. 'I wonder where it opens into the castle?' His mind was trying to catch some glimmer of memory — a faint recognition of something to do with this tunnel. He felt as if it were important for him to discover this secret back-entrance to the castle, but he didn't know why.

His curiosity got the better of him. He walked to the path along which the men had disappeared, then followed in the same direction, looking carefully to both sides. Within two minutes he saw it: a largish, grey rock about ten feet to the right of him, half buried in the earth. He went to it and was excited to discover a painted spot of white on the far side.

Eluron looked in the direction the spot was pointing to

make sure the two men were nowhere in evidence, and then he paced off thirty steps. Stooping, he glanced around him. To his left he saw a bush with some of its smaller branches broken. Beneath it he noticed that the earth seemed to be parted along two lines at right angles. He walked over and felt into the lines with his hands. His fingers touched what seemed to be the edge of a trap-door. Eluron lifted, and the door hinged upwardly to reveal a set of damp, wooden stairs leading downward.

His heart racing, he slowly descended along the stairs, soon reaching a level floor. From there a tunnel, dimly lit by occasional wall-torches, led off at a slight downward angle. Eluron listened intently for a moment, to determine whether anyone was close by in this passageway, but heard nothing but the slow staccato of dripping water echoing back and forth.

As quietly as he could, he made his way along the tunnel. At first it was internally braced with heavy timbers supporting the roof, however it soon entered into solid rock and no longer required the inside supporting structure. At length he came to a large closed wooden door, which blocked further progress along the tunnel. Eluron pressed his ear to the door and listened. From the other side came muffled voices which he could only barely make out.

"Tie her up." That sounded like a guard.

"No!" cried a woman's voice. "Let me go!"

"Over there," said another man. Eluron heard a scuffling of feet, and then a grunt from one of the men. "You witch," he groaned, "you won't soon try that again."

"No, please!" There was a dull blow and the sound of someone being dragged across the floor.

"Pull the knots extra tight," said one of the men.

Silence for a moment.

Then the other voice said, "she'll come to soon enough. Probably just in time. Korak wants to do this one personally."

Retreating footsteps, then the sound of an iron door clanking shut.

Everything was quiet now. Eluron reached out and tested

77

the wooden door. It was latched from the other side. He investigated the edges, and found that the door was separated from the opening by half an inch where the latch was located. He saw that he could probably lift the inside latch from his side if he could find some flat, long instrument like a knife. He felt around on the floor of the passageway in the dim light, and his fingers touched a shard of glass about four inches long. Gingerly he picked it up and inserted it through the crack beside the door. Then he pushed up... and the latch lifted!

The large door swung open to reveal a poorly lit room with a low ceiling and rough walls, about twenty feet square. Several chairs were scattered about, and in one of them a woman was tied up with her back to Eluron. He walked around to have a better look... it was the young Tenuli! She was unconscious and an angry red bruise on her left temple indicated exactly what had happened a moment before.

The sight of the helpless young woman, beaten and cruelly tied, filled Eluron with indignation. His normal phlegmatic disposition gave way to fury as he realized fully the cruelty and the heartlessness of the Scarlet Castle and those who ran it.

Quickly he cut the cords with the shard of glass he was still holding. Tenuli was just then regaining consciousness. "Ohh... what happened?" She looked at his face in confusion. "Eluron? What are you doing—"

"Don't try to talk. You've had a nasty blow to the temple."

"Are we alone?"

"Not for long. I heard one of the guards say that Korak himself would come down here to 'do' you, whatever that means."

"I don't want to be here to find out. How can we escape from here?"

"If Korak weren't due any moment, I'd say we should go back along the tunnel where I came in — over there." He pointed to the wooden door now standing open. "But they would easily catch us before we came to the end, unless we had a good ten minute head start. Even then they would just send a search party around the back to pick us up."

Eluron stopped to listen. The heavy footsteps of two men sounded in the distance, getting closer. "There's only one chance," he said. "We'll stand beside the iron door so that when it swings open it will hide us from sight. Then, just as it starts to open, I'll throw this piece of glass into the tunnel so they'll think we've just run in there. If we're lucky they'll rush into the tunnel, and then we can slam the door after them and latch it. That should slow them down long enough for us to reach the main floor."

With their hearts pounding they stood with their backs to the wall beside the iron door as the footsteps came closer, closer... then stopped on the other side. A key was inserted in the lock, and screeched as it turned. Slowly the large door began to creak open. Eluron waited a second, then threw the piece of glass across the room toward the tunnel-door. It banged against the edge, then clattered onto the tunnel floor about ten feet from the opening.

Just then Korak and one of his personal guards rushed into the room.

"She must be in the tunnel," said Korak. "After her!" Both of them ran into the opening and along the passageway.

Quickly Eluron stepped over to the door and slammed it shut, dropping the latch into place. Then he grabbed one of the chairs and propped it against the door. In the tunnel he heard the two men stop running, turn around, and race back toward the door.

Eluron rushed over and took Tenuli's hand. He bundled her through the open doorway leading to the castle, then pulled the iron door closed behind him. As he did so he saw the set of keys in the lock which Korak had used to open it. 'What luck,' he thought as he turned the key to seal in Korak and his guard. At the same moment he heard the tunnel door open.

Then he and Tenuli ran toward the stairs which they could see dimly at the end of the corridor.

TWENTY

Doran walked casually back toward the pantry where he had left Tenuli. He tried to plan what to do to get both of them out of the castle, but realized that he would have to rely on her knowledge of the lay-out of the building, since he was familiar with only a small part of it.

He turned into the doorway of the pantry and found it empty. His heart in his throat, he ran to the bins at the end, hoping to find her hiding in one of them. All empty!

Desperately his mind raced. What could have happened? Doubtless she had been spotted, but where would she have been taken? She had said someone called Korak had sent the two guards to get her from her room. That would mean she would now be with Korak, or confined somewhere awaiting him.

'I have to find an excuse to visit Korak,' he thought, 'and I must also find out where he is.' Doran stepped out into the corridor and walked again to the kitchen. He saw a row of freshly baked bread loaves along a counter, and an idea struck him. Confidently he walked up to the baker standing near the loaves.

"Korak's orders," he said brusquely. "Two loaves are to be taken to him immediately. Send one of your helpers to his chambers with your best loaves, some butter, and a sharp knife."

"You are not one of Korak's servants," replied the baker. "How do I know you do not just want the bread for yourself?"

"Very well. I will tell Korak you refused to obey his orders." Doran made to turn and go.

"Uh, no," said the baker quickly. "Tell him the loaves are coming." He called over to one of his helpers and explained what he had to do. The man bundled two loaves into a panier along with some butter and a knife, then walked away briskly toward the corridor that led to the stairs.

"I will tell Korak of your cooperation," said Doran as he turned to follow the helper. 'Good!' he thought to himself. 'Now I have both an excuse and a way of locating Korak's chambers.'

The baker's helper descended the staircase to the first floor level, then turned in the direction from which had come the guards sent to recapture the snakes. He then veered left down another hallway and at the end climbed a short flight of steps to a landing. Stopping before a large closed wooden door, he raised a hand to knock. At that point Doran quickly stepped forward.

"Alright," he said in a confident voice. "I'll take it from here. Korak wants me to deliver the bread personally." Obediently the helper handed over the panier, then turned and walked back along the hallway.

'Well,' thought Doran to himself, 'what now?' He stood quietly, listening for any sound from behind the door. Nothing. He knocked. No answer. He tried the handle. It was locked tight.

Doran sat down on the top step and tried to think of a plan, desperate to find his dear Tenuli. But no plan came to his mind. If only he had some clue to work with... if only he knew the basic plan of the castle. But he was helpless and he knew it.

As he sat berating himself for having failed her, a gentle face appeared to his inner eye — the kind face of Jelander. Doran remembered something the teacher had said to him before he had entered the Pathway of Change.

"She will help you to understand yourself, Doran," Jelander had said. "You do not realize how deep is your feeling for her, because in Moralia all beings have affection for all others. You think your love for her is not much different from your feeling for anyone else. But you must understand how special she is to you, and that is one of your goals for this sojourn. You will meet her at a time when she desperately needs your aid. But she will be separated from you, and you will be helpless to rescue her. Then will come a realization of how profound your feeling is for your little friend. Then you will know love in a way you have never known it before. It is right to have affection for everyone as you do, but you must also learn to love in a

81

special, personal way. One of the gifts of the Shadowland lies in its ability to separate sweethearts from each other, so that they may rise to heights of tenderness and yearning that they would never experience otherwise."

Doran thought about what Jelander had said, and then he looked inside himself, trying to understand his feelings and the ache in his heart. Tears came to his eyes. 'Now I see it,' he thought. 'Now I see it.'

Moments later he heard running footsteps along the corridor at the far end of the hallway where he was sitting. Then three guards ran past the hallway opening. Having no other plan, Doran decided to follow them at a distance, hoping they might lead him to Tenuli. Still carrying the panier, and the light of a love he had never before felt, he got up and walked quietly to the other end of the hallway.

As he turned the corner, he could hear a commotion in a large room at the end of the corridor. Through the open doorway came a din of mingled shouts, laughter and sobs. He casually approached the door, his hand on the waterpouch just in case, and then realized it was the main mess hall. Some fifty or so people were positioned at long tables with soup bowls in front of them. About half were guards, the rest regular staff. Most of the guards were holding their throats in pain, while the other people were either laughing or crying. A few were moving among the others, talking to them and comforting them.

'The soup,' thought Doran. 'It worked!'

He moved off again in the direction the three guards had taken, trying to guess where they had gone.

Then suddenly Tenuli turned a corner and came toward him. She was being helped by a man that Doran recognized as Eluron, even though they had not yet met in the Shadowland during this sojourn.

"Doran!" she cried and rushed toward him.

"Tenuli," he said softly into her hair as he put his arms around her. "What happened to you?"

"No time to explain," she replied. "This is Eluron. He got me out of one of the dungeons where I was tied up. But Korak will be after us in no time. We have to get out of the castle."

"Which way is the Great Hall?" Doran remembered their earlier discussion on the subject of escape.

"Back the way you came," she replied, leading the way.

People were beginning to spill out of the mess-hall now, some appearing delirious, others confused. A few of the guards staggered out, still clutching their throats. In the confusion and noise, nobody took any notice of Tenuli, Doran and Eluron as they made their way toward the Great Hall.

The large oaken doors to the tapestry-hung room were closed and bolted. Two guards stood at attention at either side, frowning at the three runaways as they approached. Doran realized he was still carrying the panier with the two loaves and a plan sprang into his mind. He stepped forward and said, "food to be delivered to the Great Hall. Orders from Korak."

The guards looked at them suspiciously. "Who are these other two?"

"Chief Accountant and Head of Domestic Arrangements," said Tenuli boldly. "Let us pass."

"Special war meeting going on," said one of the guards gruffly. "Orders are to let nobody in."

Doran raised the pouch and sent a jet of water at one guard, then he sprayed the other. Both of them stepped back clutching their eyes. "I can't see," cried one.

"What—? These pictures, I—," said the other.

Eluron opened the door and the three of them rushed into the Great Hall.

Fifty heads turned to look at the intruders. And the heads were on fifty fully armed bodies. It was the regiment of the Prince's own guards — known to be the meanest, toughest warriors in all of the Shadowland.

"We're sunk," said Eluron.

"No we're not," whispered Tenuli, as she turned and ran to the panels along the end wall. She reached above the fourth panel and pushed the lever. The access door fell ajar just as it had the night before. She reached out and opened it wide, hoping the sight of poisonous snakes would keep the warriors back long enough to let the three of them escape. She turned her head, listening for the expected rattling sound. None came. There were no snakes at the opening.

The armed men were getting up from their chairs now, and some were drawing their swords. "Take them!" shouted one, as several of them began to move forward. Eluron looked back at the doorway, and saw two burly guards coming through it on the run.

"Into the passageway!" he shouted. "Follow me!" Eluron had no way of knowing that this tunnel was sometimes frequented by rattlesnakes, and he had reached it and climbed in before Tenuli could speak.

"But there are snakes in there," she said to Doran.

"Can't be any worse than the vipers in this room," he said. "Here, step on my knee." Her heart pounding, she climbed up and through the open panel. Doran followed feet first so that he could guard the rear. He unstopped the pouch, then sprayed some of the water on the metal bottom of the passageway close to the entrance. 'They won't want to touch their hands on *that*,' he thought to himself. Then he passed the pouch to Tenuli and said, "give it to Eluron. Tell him to use it sparingly but to spray anything or anyone who seems evil."

Tenuli passed the message, and the three of them shuffled along the downwardly inclined passageway. Behind them, curses and shouts of pain resounded. Then the panel door slammed shut, plunging them into total darkness.

TWENTY-ONE

As they inched their way along the dark metallic tunnel, Tenuli described to the others what had happened to her when she had first opened the snake-door that same morning. "So I don't understand why there are no rattlers in here," she concluded.

"The passageway must connect with a cage or pit of some kind," speculated Doran. "Do either of you see or hear anything?"

"No." They both answered at the same time.

The three of them continued in silence.

"I'm frightened," said Tenuli.

"It'll be alright," came Doran's gentle voice.

"Something solid in front of me," said Eluron. "Like a trap door."

"Any snakes?" asked Tenuli, her voice shaking.

"No."

"Can you open the door?" said Doran.

Eluron pushed at the edges but it didn't budge. "Can't move it, but there's a crack of light underneath. Must be a room on the other side."

"Could empty right into a nest of rattlers," said Doran. "Can you turn around and hit it with your feet?"

"No. Too cramped in here."

"Okay, let's change places because I'm feet first. The tunnel seems just wide enough for us to pass each other lengthwise. I'll switch with Tenuli first, then I'll switch with you."

"Okay."

No one spoke as they changed positions. Eluron gave Doran the water pouch as they passed each other. Now Doran pulled his knees up to his chest, taking a position from where he could smash out with his feet against the door. Then he unstopped the water pouch. Little water was left now, perhaps enough for two squeezes. 'Who knows?' thought Doran to himself. 'Maybe the snakes won't like it any more than those guards.'

"Everybody ready?" he asked.

"Ready," came both voices.

"Then here goes."

With all his might Doran kicked out with his legs, forcing his feet like pile-drivers against the door. With a crash that almost deafened them in that enclosed space, the door splintered and flew inwardly. It rebounded against a glass wall, then fell to the floor. But it did not stay still. It began to shift this way and that, as the three rattlers beneath it slithered and writhed to get out from under it. Doran could see another one coiled in a far corner of the cage, which appeared to be about six feet square. The air reverberated with rattling tails.

Because of the cramped conditions in the passageway, Doran had to look down along his body to see into the cage. The bottom of the tunnel opening appeared to be about one foot up from the cage floor, and Doran realized that his legs — now protruding from the knees down — offered a tempting target for the venomous serpents. Quickly he pulled his knees up to his chest, trying to decide what to do. He knew that the water-pouch was not really much good to him, since he was not head-first toward the cage. Nor could he change his position. At the same time he didn't want to ask Tenuli or Eluron to switch with him and be the first to slide head-first onto the floor of the cage. 'We're cooked,' he said to himself.

'No,' came the gentle voice of Jelander in his mind. 'There is a way. Think.'

Doran was startled to find his teacher speaking to him telepathically, but he realized there was little time to waste on the luxury of surprise.

'Tell me how,' he pleaded in his mind.

'You have everything you need,' came the answering thought.

Doran took a mental inventory. Eluron had the set of keys that Korak had left in the door of the dungeon room where Tenuli had been tied up, and he, Doran, had the nearly empty water pouch. What else was there?

'Wait a minute!' he thought. 'The panier with the two loaves and the knife!'

"Eluron," he said out loud. "That basket with the bread. I left it about half-way along the passageway. Can you feel for it?"

"Just a moment... yes, here it is."

"Okay. I think there's a way that might get us through the snake-pit safely. Rattlers will strike at any moving target, and the bread loaves could be perfect for that. From what I recall, once a rattlesnake strikes from a coiled position, he can't immediately strike again. He has to coil up. It takes a few seconds for him to do that, and with luck one

86

of us can be out of the cage before the second strike."

There was a pause. Then Eluron took a deep breath and said, "What do you want me to do?"

"My problem is that I'm feet first, and can't switch. In order to goad the snakes into striking, I would have to be head first, like you. Are you game to do it?"

Eluron hesitated, then found the courage to say, "yes I'll do it. What's the plan?"

"Alright. First we'll switch positions again. Then you take one of the loaves and stick it on the point of the knife. Hold it by the handle and shove it repeatedly at the closest snakes that are free. Looks like two of them are still trapped under the door I kicked off, so they shouldn't be a problem unless they get free. That leaves only two other snakes that I can see from here. Let's hope there are no more around the sides out of sight.

"Now as soon as the snakes close to the opening have struck, you scramble out and try to kick open the cage door. It looks like glass with a metal edge. If it doesn't come free, just smash the glass out with the butt of the knife and then get out of the cage. We'll keep the basket and the other loaf for protection."

Tenuli had an idea. "If you and I switch, Doran, I can use the water pouch to cover Eluron. Maybe the snakes won't like the water."

Doran wrestled with the thought of exposing his dear Tenuli to such danger, but he quickly realized that they would have to use all of the weapons at their disposal, and that he, Doran, was not in a position to cover Eluron.

"I don't like it," he said. "But there is no other way. Eluron will need a hand free to work on the door, so he can't take the pouch. Are you both ready to switch?"

"Ready," said two voices.

They changed positions so that Tenuli was head-first in the second position, and Doran, still feet-first, was third.

There was a scuffling sound as Eluron fitted one of the loaves on the point of the knife. Then he said, "well, it's now or never."

"Never's a little long to wait, my friend." Doran tried to

sound jovial. "Good luck. Are you ready, Tenuli?"
"Ready."

TWENTY-TWO

With his head still inside the tunnel opening, Eluron
shoved the knife-mounted loaf at the rattlesnake coiled up
about three feet away. The noise of the rattling tails increased perceptibly. The snake raised its head a little
higher, its forked tongue flickering constantly.

He poked at the snake again...and suddenly it struck!
The long fangs penetrated deep into the crust of the bread
loaf, depositing several drops of lethal venom. Then the
snake flopped to the floor and slithered back toward a far
corner of the cage, where a second snake waited in the
coiled position.

Eluron moved forward and looked into both corners of
the cage that Doran had not been able to see. The only
other snakes were the two still trapped under the door,
though one of them had almost got free.

The coiled snake was a good five feet from the opening,
and the first one was still regrouping. Quickly Eluron
pushed his body forward, sliding into the cage on his chest
until his head was only eight inches from the loose door
under which the two snakes were still writhing.

He scrambled to his feet as Tenuli slid forward to the
tunnel opening, the water pouch held in front of her. The
coiled snake in the corner raised its head, flicking its
tongue, as Eluron stepped over the loose door and pushed
at the glass panel. It was locked. Quickly he removed the
loaf from the knife, and then smashed the handle against
the glass. Simultaneously Tenuli squirted a jet of water at
the raised head of the coiled snake, and a second at the
first snake which had now coiled itself up again. Both of
the reptiles instantly dropped their heads and began squir-
ming as if in pain.

The first blow against the glass failed to have any effect.
Eluron smashed again, harder this time, and the glass disin-

tegrated into a hundred shards that clattered out onto the floor of the room.

Tenuli aimed at the head of one of the snakes that had just worked its way free of the door, and squeezed. The pouch was empty. A few drops fell harmlessly to the floor of the cage.

"Look out behind you!" she screamed as Eluron bent to clear away the remaining fragments of glass sticking in the metal frame. He turned to see the coiled snake raise its head into position... but it never completed its strike. Tenuli had scrambled into the cage and grabbed the neck of the snake from behind. The powerful serpent body writhed about her arms as the reptile struggled to free itself. "Here!" she said, holding the head down against the cage floor. Eluron turned and plunged the knife-point into the skull of the rattlesnake. The beast flopped lifeless to the floor.

"Ugh!" exclaimed Tenuli, excited and revulsed at the same time. She had acted instinctively to protect Eluron, and only afterward did she realize fully what she had done.

"Quickly!" said Doran as he slid feet-first into the cage. "Finish the last one too!"

Eluron bent and with a quick slash he severed the head of the fourth snake where it poked out from under the loose door.

Then all three of them jumped through the smashed opening and onto the floor of the room.

"What place is this?" Doran looked at the glassware and bottles of chemicals lining the high shelves.

"I don't know this room," answered Tenuli.

"Wait a minute!" came Eluron's voice. "I got into the castle by following two men who were talking about a laboratory of some kind. Maybe this is it. They were bringing in two large bags of water from the Well of Tears."

"Water from the Well of Tears? Why?" asked Doran.

"They were talking about finding some way to neutralize it. Judging by the effect of your water-pouch on the snakes and the guards, it must be a potent weapon."

Doran laughed. "It's not really meant as a weapon,

Eluron," he said. "It was intended to help us remember why we have come to the land of shadows. But if it touches someone — or something — that is outright evil, it will burn them the way it did the snakes."

"Have you never drunk the water?" asked Tenuli.

"No. Not that I recall."

"Well, we'll get some for you first chance we have," chuckled Doran, giving Eluron a friendly slap on the back.

"Look over here," came Tenuli's voice from a corner of the room. "Did you say two water bags?"

"Yes."

"Well, I think I've found them!"

Doran and Eluron ran over to Tenuli. "Looks like the same ones they were carrying," confirmed Eluron, as he inspected the large bags lying on a bench.

"Let's fill the pouch," said Tenuli, "and maybe some of these empty glass bottles. And Eluron should drink some, too."

"Wait," said Doran. "Maybe they've doctored the water in some way. Poisoned it or something. Let me taste it first." He took the stopper from the mouth of one of the large bags, spilled some into his cupped hand, and tasted it with his tongue. Nothing happened. No pictures in his mind. No increased memory of Moralia. He drank a small sip. Still nothing.

"I don't know," he said. "It tastes like normal water, but the memory effect doesn't happen."

"Let me try," said Tenuli, taking some into her cupped hand.

Just then they heard footsteps outside the door of the laboratory. "We did just as Korak suggested," came a man's voice. "We put a small amount of rattlesnake venom into one of the water pouches, and the water no longer hurt the snakes when it touched them."

Tenuli, Doran and Eluron ducked behind a large set of lined shelves set about two feet from the wall.

"So the water is now poison to drink?" said another man's voice.

"No. The venom is lethal only when in the bloodstream.

90

If you swallow it, the digestive juices break it down into harmless components."

A key turned in the lock and the door swung open.

"What about the other water bag?" A tall, thin man entered the laboratory.

"Haven't touched it yet," said the other, following the first through the door. "We're planning to use it to see just how dilute the venom can be and still render the water harml—"

"Hey!" said the first one. "The snake cage! Looks like the door's been smashed from the inside. Maybe whoever did it is still in—"

He got no more words out. Doran grabbed him from behind as Tenuli rushed to the second water bag with the knife. She slashed it open, caught some in an empty glass jar from a nearby shelf, then dashed it in the man's face. He shouted and collapsed at Doran's feet. The other man bolted through the door, closing it behind him and turning the key.

"The guards'll be swarming over this room in seconds," shouted Doran. "Quick! Fill the pouch and several glass bottles from the second bag. Eluron, try your keys! See if you can open that door!"

Eluron rushed to the door as Doran and Tenuli began filling containers. Much of the water had already spilled out through the knife-cut onto the laboratory floor, but there was enough left for their needs.

"It's open!" shouted Eluron, as he swung the door wide.

"Let's go!" said Doran. He ran out carrying two bottles of well water, and realized he was in the main corridor which led to the Great hall.

"Which way?" asked Eluron, following close behind.

"The horses are all kept in the foreyard in front of the main entrance," said Tenuli. "Our best chance is straight through the Great Hall." Doran began to run ahead. The other two followed closely, armed with as many containers as they could carry.

"Hey you three!" A guard saw them and gave chase. He

was quickly joined by two others. Tenuli swung one of her bottles and water sprayed all three of the guards. They shouted in surprise and stopped.

A number of people were wandering aimlessly through the castle halls, while others were sitting in confusion on the floor. Doran recognized them as the ones who had tasted the 'magic' soup, and suddenly he had an idea. "Listen all of you!" he shouted loudly as he ran. "This castle is not the place for you. It's a trap! Don't be duped by Korak and his bunch. Escape with us! Your strength is needed in the fight against evil!"

The words rang up and down the corridor, punctuated by their running footsteps. Many of the wanderers stopped and listened, their look of confusion clearing away.

"Yes," they began to say. "He's right. We don't belong in this place." They started to follow the three runaways, and soon a whole crowd of awakened people were pounding down the corridor and into the Great Hall.

None of the Prince's warriors was in the enormous room, empty now except for a few disoriented staff members leaning against the walls and holding their heads.

"Join us!" shouted the crowd as it surged toward the main gate, which was locked. Eluron moved to the front with his keys and quickly found the one which opened the way.

Doran sprinted ahead, sending jets of water into the faces of the few guards and horse-grooms who were in the stable area along one side of the foreyard. The guards staggered back covering their eyes, but the grooms remembered quickly and began to help prepare the horses for the escape.

Everyone had mounted up inside of ten minutes. Doran, Eluron and Tenuli charged out of the foreyard and headed down the road away from the castle, with some forty riders thundering behind them.

"Do you know the way to the Knight's stronghold?" Doran shouted to Tenuli.

"No, but I can get us to the hunting cabins that his followers sometimes use as a lay-over," she called back.

92

"Take the left fork ahead!"

Doran signalled okay with his fingers, then spurred his horse to a full gallop. He swerved left at the fork, and the rest pounded behind him as he headed west.

* * *

In Moralia, Jelander watched the riders. "Eluron has yet to drink the water," he remarked.

"Yes," replied Trillamar. "I have influenced matters such that his tasting of the water would be delayed. He refused to drink from the Well of Tears when he first arrived in the Shadowland, thus turning his back on the help it might have given him. The result of that refusal must be to withold the water's illumination from him a little longer."

"Even so," said Jelander, "he is turning to the side of truth and light. It may be that, deep down, he wanted to show himself that he could choose the right without any dependence on the well water."

"When this sojourn is over," concluded Trillamar, "Eluron will know truth unerringly from within. In time, all Moralians must do the same."

"It will come to pass," answered Jelander.

* * *

That evening, the band of riders made a rough camp by the side of the road. A fire was lit, and a sparse meal was cooked from some of the emergency provisions which they discovered in the saddlebags. All were exhausted and most of them found spots on the ground where they could catch a few hours of needed rest.

Tenuli and Doran lay close to each other on a padding of leaves that he had gathered. Doran drifted off to sleep, but though Tenuli was also tired she was still too excited by the events of the day to close her eyes. As the campfire died away, she lay on her back and watched the bits of burning ash float skyward, glowing like tiny fitful lights against the blackness. They drifted up, up... then blinked out. Drifting, disappearing…no — there was one that did not disappear. What was that? Her eyes fixed on a steady pin-prick of light glowing in the sky — a clear, unwavering dot of illumination.

Tenuli raised herself to a sitting position and looked again, but the tiny spot was gone. For the second time in as many days, the thick layer of cloud had briefly parted. And again the purity of starlight had fallen upon the land of shadows.

TWENTY-THREE

Toth had organized most of the Knight's followers into bands of ten men each, these being the ones who would wait just outside the army encampment until the riders arrived from Sandria with the water bags.

A core group had also been established, which included those who would make the initial raid on the well — to seize it from the Prince's men — as well as those who would actually ride with the water bags into the army encampment. Specifically, Toth, Fromil and the Silent One were to make the first raid. Toth was also to lead the group of five bag riders because his horse was one of the largest and fastest. He would be accompanied by the Silent One, known for his great courage, and by Sindor, who was light in weight. The other two positions had yet to be filled.

News had come from the scouts at Sandria that the Prince's army was assembling only three miles north-west from the town. Many tents had been erected, and several battalions had been observed in military drill. Supplies were being moved in from the Grey City.

The Knight had decided to launch his campaign without further delay, and so he, Toth and the rest of the men had set off eastward from the Redwood Forest, heading for the hunting cabins about one day's ride away.

The journey went without incident, and toward dusk the riders pulled up at the cabins. Most had to sleep outside, of course, and a number of lean-tos were erected for shelter. Drinking water was obtained from a nearby spring, and the men busied themselves with their horses and the cooking of a simple meal over the inside woodstoves.

Toth, Fromil and the Silent One met together with the Knight after they had finished eating.

"Tomorrow is the day," said the Knight. "Our scouts say that the security force around the well has doubled. The Prince will send his most trusted guards to destroy it very soon, and we must try to gain control of it before he does so."

"But what if he starts tomorrow morning?"

"I don't think that will happen. Our information is that a heavily guarded carriage left the Prince's Northern Outpost yesterday, heading in the direction of the army encampment. We believe it is bringing the Prince of Shades himself. It will not arrive before late tomorrow, and it is unlikely that the order to attack the well will be given until the Prince is in the camp. His vanity would not allow him to miss what he thinks will be his greatest victory."

Events seemed to bear out the Knight's assumptions, for no attack upon the well came that night or during the next morning.

Around midday, Toth heard the distant sound of many riders approaching. He rushed to report it to the Knight. "Horses!" he exclaimed. "Sounds like at least thirty. Probably a regiment of guards from the castle!"

"Send look-outs," said the Knight. "Tell the men to prepare for a fight." Toth gave the necessary orders, then he took the Silent One and ten more of the strongest fighters to an ambush position about one hundred yards up the road. They hid behind the bushes, unstopped their large water pouches, and waited.

Up the road came Doran, Tenuli, Eluron and the other riders, looking slightly bedraggled for having slept on hard ground the previous night. Toth realized that, although the horses certainly belonged to the Prince of Shades, the people riding on them were far from constituting a regiment of soldiers. Then he recognized the girl he had found on the ground in Sandria.

Smiling, he stood and walked out into full view. "Tenuli!" he called. Doran held up a hand to halt the cavalcade.

"It's alright," Tenuli called over. "That's Toth. He is a follower of the Knight of Roses." Though her heart had jumped at the sight of the young man, she quickly realized that her true affection was for Doran. But she couldn't think about those matters now. She dismounted and walked toward Toth.

"We escaped from the Scarlet Castle yesterday afternoon," she explained. "We had hoped to find some of the Knight's men here, so that we could offer to join them. Are you alone?"

Toth laughed, then hugged Tenuli in welcome. "Alone?" he said. "There are almost a hundred of us here, and this evening we will be in control of the Well of Tears." He turned to address the rest of the riders. "Any of you who wish to serve the Knight of Roses will get your chance," he said. "We need people who know the truth and are willing to explain it to others."

Most of the riders dismounted and approached him to offer their help. Toth called one of the fighters forward from behind the bush, and put him in charge of the volunteers. Then Doran and Eluron got down from their horses and were introduced to Toth.

"They are just the bravest men I've ever met," said Tenuli to Toth. Then she remembered Toth's own courage and added, "aside from you, of course...and the Silent One ...and, and—"

"Never mind," laughed Toth. "We have lots of room for bravery here." He shook hands with Doran and Eluron, and then quickly explained to them the plan that the Knight would soon put into motion.

Next, all four of them met with the Knight of Roses in one of the cabins. The three who had escaped from the castle took an instant liking to this quiet-spoken man, feeling instinctively that his motives were totally pure, and that he acted only from a desire to restore the light of Moralia to the Shadowland.

"Toth has already explained the basic plan to you?" asked the Knight.

"Yes," answered Doran, "but there is something that you should know. The Prince has discovered that by mixing rattlesnake venom with the well water, it loses its effect and reverts to normal water. We tasted some that had been treated with the venom, and it had no power to restore any memory. Apparently, it also failed to 'burn' some rattlesnakes that were subjected to it. Perhaps the Prince will try to dump some of the venom into the well. I think only a little is required."

"I see," said the Knight. "That is bad news indeed. We had assumed he would simply try to fill in the well."

Toth said, "we will have to watch carefully for someone trying to throw a container of liquid into the Well of Tears."

"Yes," replied the Knight. "Tell the men to be on their guard." Toth nodded agreement.

There was a sharp rap on the cabin door. Then Fromil entered and said, "it's Sindor. He's on his horse galloping toward Sandria."

"Why did he go?"

"All day he has been agitated. He spent much of the night sharpening his dagger. I fear he means to take some rash action."

"That could jeopardize our whole plan," said the Knight. "He must be overtaken."

"I'll go," said Toth. "My horse is very fast. I should be able to catch him before he reaches the town." With that he ran out of the cabin.

"This means we shall need someone else to ride with a water pouch into the army camp," said the Knight, half to himself. "Sindor cannot be trusted to remain in control of himself."

"Let me do it." Tenuli rose and looked at the Knight of Roses. "I can ride well, and I weigh less than any of your men."

"No," said Doran. "It's too dangerous..."

But the Knight smiled at her. "I have heard a little of your

97

recent adventures," he said, "and I gather that you have more than your share of courage. If you really wish to volunteer, then we shall be happy to accept."

Doran realized that it would be pointless to argue with her, so he said, "if you are to ride into the camp, then I wish to offer as well." He turned to look at the Knight.

"Let me go too," said Eluron, surprised at his own courage.

"You shall all go together," laughed the Knight, "along with Toth and the Silent One. Anyone who can escape from the castle by sliding through a cage full of rattlesnakes, and then bring half the staff with them, should have little difficulty with a mere battalion or so of armed warriors!"

"Then it's settled," said Tenuli.

A short time later, Toth and Sindor returned to the hunting cabins. Only minutes from the edge of Sandria, Toth had spotted Sindor ahead of him, waving his unsheathed dagger like a wild man. Toth had ridden up behind the other's horse, then had jumped over to bring Sindor crashing to the ground. Both of them had been badly bruised in the fall, but the shake-up had cleared Sindor's head so that Toth could persuade him to return to the hunting cabins.

Soon after, it was time to carry the Knight's plan into effect. Most of the men set out for the army encampment to take up positions in the neighboring forest, while the selected party of ten riders mounted up and headed for the edge of Sandria. Toth, Fromil and the Silent One led the way. The Knight rode behind Toth, with Doran and Eluron in a line behind him. Tenuli kept pace beside Doran, and behind her rode Blenik and two other fast riders. Blenik had been chosen because of his familiarity with the routine of the Prince's guards.

The trip to Sandria took only about one hour. The Knight halted them just outside the town, still under cover of the woods. "The path we have followed to here is not well known to the Prince's men," he said. "Luckily we have encountered nobody. But from here on, take great care.

The town is probably crawling with them."

They split up. Toth, Fromil and the Silent One went left, and the rest angled right. They had agreed that Toth's group would station itself at the north edge of Sandria, while the Knight and the others would stop about half a mile to the west of town, still inside the woods, where they would start a fire to heat the rocks.

Eluron was to ride in closer and take up a hidden position near the main square, from where he could watch any activity at the Well of Tears. As soon as he saw that Toth and the others had secured the well, he was to ride back and report to the Knight, whereupon all the rest — including Eluron — would head for the well with the heated rocks and the other three large water bags (Toth and the Silent One would have their two bags already at the well). As soon as all the bags could be filled, the five 'bag-riders' would gallop off toward the army encampment.

Everything was ready.

Everyone was poised for action.

In the camp, Korak stopped in front of a medium-sized black tent.

"Enter, Korak," said a deep bass voice.

Korak walked through the flaps of the tent. "Sir," he said, "we have found the antidote for the Well of Tears." He placed a small dark bottle into the hands of the Prince of Shades.

A small dark bottle filled with rattlesnake venom.

TWENTY-FOUR

Eluron left his horse tied to a tree at the outskirts of town, then walked toward what appeared to be a disused silo of some kind. The cylindrical stone building stood in full view of the Well of Tears, but from within it Eluron would not be seen. He approached an opening at ground level, where a broken door was hanging from one hinge. Moving it aside, he peered into the silo. In the dim light he could make out a rickety ladder stretching upwardly. He entered the structure and saw that the top of the ladder was near the broken roof of the silo, about fifteen feet up.

Eluron climbed slowly, testing each rung as he went. All of them held. At the top he reached up and pushed on one of the loose roof-boards. It yielded and he was able to wedge it over to one side so that his view of the Well of Tears would be unobstructed.

He had brought with him a pouch of the well water (which he had not yet tasted), and a dagger. Eluron found the weapon repulsive, as he had never had an aggressive or belligerant disposition. Indeed, his nature — if he were to admit the truth — was deeply introspective and insular. He tended to prefer isolation to crowds, sober thought to frivolity.

And yet, as his mind went back over the events of the past two days, he realized that deep sea-changes were taking place within his being. He had agreed to oversee the Prince's finances because of personal motives which were less than completely honorable: he had wanted to have and be around wealth. But when he had encountered Tenuli, a different cast of thought had started to invade his mind. He began to notice innuendos of iniquity to which he had previously turned a blind eye. Events which he had earlier interpreted benignly now assumed a darker shading, and he began to see the Scarlet Castle for what it really was: a crucible of evil that seduced Shadowlanders into betraying their best selves for the sake of unworthy motives.

His eyes had first been opened when Korak had heartlessly condemned the jailer to be tortured in the 'Chamber of Cooperation'. Then, when he had found poor Tenuli bound and beaten in the dungeon room, it was as if something had clicked open in his mind. He suddenly realized not only the manifest danger of remaining in the castle, but the true dimensions of the wickedness that brooded over that place.

Subsequently, as he, Tenuli and Doran had struggled to escape, the necessity for courage and action had drawn qualities from him that he had not suspected were there. The episode in the rattlesnake cage had totally changed his perception of himself. He saw that he could be brave in the face of danger, resourceful when obstacles blocked the way. And that realization triggered feelings of worthiness and self-respect that for long had been buried under impenetrable layers of melancholy and gloom.

Excitement filled him now as he watched the scene around the Well of Tears. Three of the Prince's guards were near it, standing with their backs to the wall and their swords drawn. Further away, another five guards were sitting on the ground near a small tent which had been set up on the square. Eluron assumed that they were now off-duty, and that some sort of rotating system had been established to ensure that the well would be always under guard.

The group of eight guards was under full armor, and Eluron strained to make out the details of the protective garb they were wearing. The helmets were black, with horns at either side. The movable visors, when pulled down, covered the eyes and nose but left the mouth and chin exposed. A tunic and leggings of scarlet cloth were partly covered by a black metal breastplate and another metal plate girdling the loins. Each guard had a sword and shield, the latter being painted with a diagonal stripe of grey against a scarlet background, with a black horned circle — the 'dead sun' — in the middle. The three guards on active duty also had long black lances. Eluron shivered at the thought of being impaled on those evil-looking shafts.

Suddenly he heard pounding hooves, and from the opposite side of the square came Toth, Fromil and the Silent One, riding toward the well at full gallop. Toth was in the lead, holding a large hand-pouch full of water. From a distance of twenty feet he began to spray the closest guard, who had raised his sword to strike. The guard reached up and quickly pulled his visor down over his eyes. The water struck the guard on the head and one hand, and he jumped back to avoid being hit again. At the same time he swung his sword, but Toth swerved and easily avoided the blade. Another jet struck the guard, this time on his exposed neck. He stumbled and fell to the ground, clutching his throat.

Meanwhile the other two guards were under attack from Fromil and the Silent One. Fromil rode past, splattering them both lightly with water, but the Silent One lept off his horse at one of them, seizing the man's wrist and pinning him to the ground. Neither guard had had sufficient time to pull his visor down over his face, and now Toth had ridden over and dowsed them both. One of them convulsed in pain, but the other one — the man being held down by the Silent One — merely looked surprised and confused. The Silent One let the guard up, and Fromil began talking earnestly to him.

Then the Silent One went to the well and began to crank the capstan around which the bucket rope was wound. But the rope oscillated loosely, and even Eluron from his distance could see that there was no weight at the bottom of it. The cut end came into sight, and Toth ran over to look into the well. He pointed down excitedly and said something to the others that Eluron could not hear. Then Toth motioned to the crank, grabbed the rope, and lept up onto the wall of the well. The Silent One slowly rotated the crank and lowered Toth down out of sight.

By this time the other five guards had almost covered the distance from the tent to the well. They ran with their swords drawn, but stopped about twenty feet away, just beyond the range of the water jet which Fromil was directing at them.

Eluron decided that it was time to ride back to where the Knight was waiting. Toth and the others seemed to be in control of the well, but it appeared that they might need reinforcements quickly. The ladder creaked as Eluron climbed down it. Then he turned to leave the silo.

The hulking figure in the doorway said, "well, my friend, so we meet again!" His heart sinking, Eluron looked up into the face of Hindalom.

The Knight of Roses paced back and forth in front of the fire, while Doran watched the large rocks they had positioned close to its base. From time to time the Knight glanced worriedly in the direction of Sandria.

"Toth must have started the raid by now," he said to Doran. "Darkness is less than an hour away."

"Yes," agreed the other. "Should we not load the rocks and move closer? Something may be delaying Eluron."

The Knight thought a moment, then said, "you are right, Doran. Eluron was armed with water and a weapon, but he could have been taken by surprise and been unable to use either." He then called to the others and instructed everyone to mount up. Doran adjusted the asbestos side-pockets he had rigged on his horse, and then used water soaked gloves to transfer the hot rocks. The hissing steam startled the animal, who shied away momentarily. But the rocks were soon safely in the pockets, and Doran swung up into the saddle.

The Knight's horse pranced impatiently as he addressed the rest of the riders. "We must all sweep in at once," he said. "Doran and I will be in the lead. Use your pouches if anyone tries to stop you. Remember why you are doing this... and good luck!"

With that he spurred his horse forward, followed by Doran and the others. A minute later they saw a rider galloping toward them. It was Eluron, who waved wildly as they reined up.

"What news?" shouted the Knight, pulling to a stop.

"One of the stalkers tried to stop me," answered Eluron, "but I knew him from before, and persuaded him that I was still loyal to the Prince of Shades. Then I offered him a drink of water, which he accepted." Eluron laughed. "I bet he's still sitting on the ground, shaking his head."

"What about Toth and the others?"

"They're at the well, but the bucket's been cut from the rope. I think Toth saw it down the well, and went in after it. But more guards were converging on them when I encountered the stalker."

"Alright. We're riding in now. Better use your pouches

103

sparingly. We may have to pour our own water on the rocks until the bucket can be rigged up again."

"Let's go!" They spurred their mounts to full gallop.

Toth looked down into the clear, dark water below as the Silent One lowered him into the Well of Tears. He smiled as the closeness of that wonderful liquid filled his heart with a lightness that even the Redwood Forest could not match. Bracing his legs against one side of the well and his shoulder against the other, he reached down and grasped the handle of the wooden bucket where it bobbed at the water's surface.

"Okay!" he shouted up to the Silent One, banging the taut rope with his hand. The latter started to turn the crank, gradually pulling Toth up. His head appeared above the wall. "Here it is!" he said, smiling, "Looks like someone used a knife. With luck we can attach it so that the rope is still long enough." He climbed out. "Where are those other guards?"

"They retreated to the tent," answered Fromil. "Then one of them rode off in the direction of the encampment."

"That should bring the crack troops on the double," said Toth. "We haven't much time." Quickly he tied the bucket to the severed end of the rope, then tossed it down the well. The Silent One grasped the rope and pulled it in hand over hand, a faster process than cranking. The bucket came up filled with well water, and Fromil began reloading their half-empty pouches from it. Then he started to fill the large water bag strapped to Toth's horse.

The guard who had not been burned by the water seemed now to have cleared his head. He got up and approached Toth. "I came to the Shadowland," he said, "to learn compassion for others. The water made me remember that. But I have followed a heartless path by joining the Prince's guards. I have failed."

Toth smiled at the man. "No, my friend," he said. "Sometimes we learn the lessons better if we explore all the darker pathways first. By falling into error, we see the true dimensions of the climb we must make back into the light.

104

For some of us, that is the only way to succeed in the lower world."

The man looked gratefully at Toth. "Thank you," he said simply.

"What is your name?"

"Stentor."

"The Prince will soon do his best to destroy this well, Stentor," said Toth. "If you join us, his chances will be that much less. Are you willing?"

Stentor grinned and grasped the handle of his sword. "They say that I am good with my blade."

"Swords and daggers are a last resort with us," answered Toth. "Our goal is to persuade the Prince's men to join us as you have done, by using the water from the Well of Tears. Can you learn a gentler way than the clash of steel?"

"I can," replied Stentor. "I can."

Pounding hooves sounded in the distance, as the seven riders came into sight. The four remaining guards at the tent drew their swords, but backed away before the rush of the powerful horses. The riders reined up at the well and dismounted. Doran removed the rocks and set them on the ground beside the well. Immediately Fromil began to drop water on the hot surface, and it hissed as clouds of vapour billowed up around them. Luckily there was little wind, and the vapour spread out equally in all directions.

"What news?" asked the Knight.

"Additional troops should arrive at any moment," said Toth. "One of the well guards rode off to the army camp soon after we got here."

"The vapour should slow them down," answered the Knight.

"The two water bags we brought in have been filled," called Fromil over the hiss of the steam.

"We'll fill the other three," said Doran, as he and Eluron busied themselves with the large bags that they and Tenuli had brought to the well.

The daylight had now dimmed perceptibly, and it was imperative that the five bag-riders leave for the camp as soon as possible.

Suddenly everyone stopped what they were doing and strained to listen. Their faces turned toward each other in question, then their eyes searched the distant gathering darkness for some clue. Octaves beneath the sibilant hissing of the steam, a deep bass sound had rolled over them — a deep bass sound like the muffled boom of a thousand cannon from a thousand miles away — a deep bass sound like the voice of a mountain calling to the sea.

Then came the quivering pulse beneath their feet as the earth shook. The horses pranced and whinnied in sudden fear... and then just as suddenly the quake was over.

"What was *that*?" asked Doran.

"Don't think I want to know," answered Blenik.

"Whatever it was," said the Knight, sounding as confident as he could, "it's over now. Probably just some freak natural occurrence. How are those bags coming?"

"Just finishing the last one," called Eluron.

"Alright everyone," said the knight. "It'll be dark in twenty minutes — so dark you won't be able to see your hand in front of your face. Toth knows the way, so follow him in single file. And trust the horses — they can find the path even when you can't see it. Stay down close to your horses' necks because some of the branches are very low. When we get to the camp, Toth will direct each of you bag-riders to one of the fires. Remember to use your water pouches on anyone who gets in your way. That camp'll be in total pandemonium within a minute of our entry, and you will be in great danger — especially from the leaders like Korak. Our men will move in quickly from the nearby woods, but you five will be the first ones there and highly visible against the campfires.

"The rest of us in this group will be close behind you, but we will dismount and move into the camp on foot. Fromil, the Silent One and I will storm the tent that looks like the headquarters, in the hopes of catching Korak or the Prince before they can escape.

"Remember why you are doing this, and remember that the Great Light is with you and within you. Good luck —

and let's get going!"

The Knight and Toth mounted up and waited a moment to make sure that all of the others were ready. Eluron checked the straps on his water bag, then stepped into the stirrup. Doran went over to help Tenuli onto her horse. As she started to swing up into the saddle, the horse shied and she lost her balance. Doran managed to catch her as she fell.

"What's wrong with that horse?" called Toth.

"Mine's skitterish too," said Fromil. "Hey! What's that—?"

The deep bass sound rolled over them again as the horses pranced nervously. The earth quivered and from close by came a dull crash as one wall of the grey brick building at the edge of the square collapsed. There were shouts of surprise and pain from the same direction, and then another sustained booming roar — much louder than the others — filled the reverberating air.

"It's coming from *here*!" shouted Toth. "From the *well itself*! We've got to get out of here!"

As the boom died away, they heard the hooves of galloping horses approaching. Against the gathering darkness they could make out three warriors, all heavily armored, riding straight toward them from the edge of the square. Two were slightly ahead, swinging their unsheathed sabres. The third carried a small, dark bottle in his left hand.

"Fall back!" shouted Toth. "The water won't get through that armor! Split up so they have more than one target!"

But the warriors did not swerve as Toth and the others spread out. They continued in a straight line directly toward the stone wall of the Well of Tears.

Suddenly the earth began to shake violently again. The rest of the grey brick building collapsed with a roar as the third warrior raised high the bottle of venom, then hurled it with all his strength as he thundered past. Toth heard the sound of the bottle smashing against stone, then he gasped as the earth around the well caved in and the three warriors plunged screaming into the gaping hole. At the same moment the well itself started to rise up out of the

107

ground, quivering and vibrating like an iron bar struck with a hammer. Now above the booming voice of the earthquake a new sound could be heard — a long sustained OM-M-M...like the chanting of a hundred thousand human voices holding a single note of power and praise.

The well had now risen over thirty feet. Dirt and small stones were tumbling down into the chasm from the damp wall newly exposed to the air, as the shaft of rock continued to rise and reverberate.

The Knight signalled to the others who were still spread out around the square, trying to control their mounts. "Listen all of you! This whole town could explode at any moment," he shouted. "I don't know what this is, but we have to get away from it! Ride for the encampment as we had planned!"

Toth and the Knight spurred their horses to a full gallop. Doran, Tenuli and the others followed. Except for the Silent One, who feared nothing, they were all as frightened by the supernatural behavior of the Well of Tears as they were by the dangerous prospects that lay before them.

When they were half-way to the camp, the rising column of the Well of Tears — now over fifteen hundred feet in the air — exploded. The magic water streamed out and into the surrounding cloud layer, making them heavy with added moisture. The rocky fragments of the disintegrated wall tumbled down into the gaping chasm where the well had been, and when the last pebble had been swallowed up, the earth closed. The Well of Tears was no more.

But Tenuli knew nothing of the miraculous events back at Sandria. She leaned close to her horse's neck as the branches brushed and scraped against her body, trying to hold onto the mane to keep herself from falling. Ahead of her was Doran, and Toth was in front of him leading the way. She didn't know the order of the horses behind her. It was now pitch black and her heart pounded in fear that she would be ripped off the saddle by a tree or branch that she wouldn't even see before it struck.

But the horse seemed to know the way, and to sense the

position of the other animals. Toth shouted something, and Doran relayed the message. "It's just ahead," he called back, "start to rein in slowly."

From behind her she heard the Knight's voice shout the same message to the others. As Tenuli pulled gently on the reins, she caught sight of distant flames flickering through the branches of the trees. Seconds later, they were close enough to see each other dimly by the light of the five campfires. They reined to a halt at the forest edge, and strained to make out the activity on the huge plain stretching before them. Men were moving to and fro near the fires, and they could see a neat row of tents off to one side. A little further away was a large structure that looked like a mess-hall, and a few supply tents were scattered near one of the fires. They did not notice the black tent at the far end of the camp, for it reflected no light at all.

"Okay," called Toth, "we'll be spotted any moment. Doran, you take the closest fire; Tenuli, you have the one right beside it. Eluron, you go for that big fire by the mess-hall. The Silent One and I will take the far ones along the other edge of camp. Get out your blades, and remember to ride across the edge of the fire. The horses will not be burned because the contact will be brief. Let's go!"

Tenuli spurred to a gallop and headed for the fire Toth had indicated. Her knuckles whitened as she gripped the reins with her left hand and the dagger with the right. Waves of fear rose from her stomach and her heart pounded in her throat as the fire loomed up. Suddenly clouds of acrid smoke engulfed her as she struggled to keep her frightened horse from shying away from the flames. She blinked her eyes to clear away the stinging, and realized she should have circled out a bit so as not to approach the fire from directly downwind. 'Too late to change now,' she thought, 'here goes!' The horse's hooves slammed into the burning embers at the edge of the fire. At the same moment she slashed at the bag with her dagger. Water gushed over part of the fire's base, sending clouds of steam, smoke and ash billowing up behind her. Shouts and cries were coming from all over the camp now, as the officers tried

109

to organize their men. Tenuli pulled out the water pouch and sprayed it liberally before her, spurring her horse to follow Doran — who had just dowsed his own fire.

"Tenuli!" he called back to her. "Toth is down off his horse. I'm going in to help him. Try to find the Silent One and stay with him. He'll get you to safety."

"No!" she shouted. "My duty is here with you and the others. I'm going to look for Korak. I've seen him more recently than the rest of you, and I'll recognize him more easily in this light."

"Tenuli—" Suddenly their two horses swerved in opposite directions to avoid one of the fires that was still partly burning, and Tenuli found herself alone, galloping straight toward the small black tent at the edge of camp. She pulled on the reins with all her strength and the horse came to a prancing stop — right in front of the black canvas flaps.

Every shred of intuition within her screamed that she should flee this place at once — that the supremest evil that ever existed was waiting within the tent before her. Yet she made no move to escape. Instead, as if in some nightmarish dream, she got down off the horse and waited. Behind her the shouts of confusion and laughter blended into a background din that she seemed not to hear.

"Tenuli," said a deep bass voice from within the black tent. "I have been expecting you."

TWENTY—FIVE

A black-gloved hand reached through the tent flaps and parted them. "Come, Tenuli," said the bass voice within the tent. "Surely you wish to see what I look like?"

Her stomach was a tight ball of fear, but somehow she found her footsteps approaching the tent. "Yes," she whispered hoarsely through a constricted throat. "Yes, I want to see you." She unstopped the nozzle of the water pouch hanging at her side.

"No need for that," said the deep bass voice. "The well

water has no effect on me."

Now as curious as she was frightened, Tenuli stepped through the tent flaps and looked directly at the figure standing before her.

Doran's face smiled back.

Tenuli gasped as her mind reeled. "Doran? *Doran?*" She could hardly say the name. Then as she watched in horror, the features of the face changed and melted into a resemblance of Toth. She gathered all of her self-control and fought down the waves of nausea that were rising from the pit of her stomach. Then she took a deep breath, raised the water pouch, and squeezed. The jet of liquid passed straight through the Prince of Shades as if he were a ghost, and splattered against the far wall of the tent.

"I told you the water would be of no effect," laughed the Prince of Shades with Toth's face. "Now sit down and ask me what you wish to know." The face melted again and darkened. In its place there was only a featureless, shadowy blur.

Tenuli sat down in a small camp chair, feeling suddenly very weak in the knees.

"Well?" said the deep bass voice.

She summoned up all of her self-control and said, "why do you not destroy me as you have so many others?"

"You slander me, Tenuli," said the Prince. "I have destroyed no one. It is they who bring about their own destruction."

"But the prisoners in the dungeons — Doran said they had been horribly tortured..."

"All of their pain has been inflicted by other Shadowlanders," replied the Prince. "I do not sully myself with that business."

"What about the slaves that built the castle? They were whipped and beaten."

"The slave-drivers were all Shadowlanders," answered the Prince. "I gave them the opportunity to indulge their cruel natures, and they did the rest."

"Are you saying you are not guilty for any of the pain and destruction in this forsaken land?"

"Guilt is totally foreign to my purpose," came the reply. "You have not understood yet what I am."

"Are you not from the place which the water makes me remember?"

"No."

"Then what in the name of damnation are you?"

The Prince did not reply. Instead, the grey blur of his head gradually changed and moved until... *Tenuli's own face peered back at her!* She gasped, and then regained control of herself — deciding that this was a mere trick to frighten her.

"No," said the Prince, reading her thoughts. "Not to frighten you. To show you what I am."

"You're... you're *me?*" She hardly understood the question she had just asked.

"In a sense, I am you," answered the Prince of Shades as his face returned to a formless blur. "I am like a distillation of the true, essential nature of every person in this land. That is why I can show the face of anyone. Now do you see?"

Outside, large droplets of rain began to fall, as Tenuli struggled to grasp what she was dealing with. But then her practical nature took control. She realized there was one thing she did not understand at all. "Why are you taking the trouble to explain all this to me?" she asked boldly.

"Tenuli," answered the voice, "I am much misunderstood. My role in this land is merely to make it possible for people to do what their true natures dictate. The pain and darkness you have seen about you has arisen simply because most of those who came here were motivated by baseness and selfish desires. It is not my fault that I was given inferior raw material to work with."

The rain was falling harder now, splattering against the canvas roof and creating a fine mist within the tent as the Prince continued.

"But you are different, Tenuli," he said. "You wish to see changes here — changes for the better. I can help you realize that positive goal, just as I have abetted the negative aims of others. You are a clever organizer, and I can bring you opportunities to do the things you want. Together we could lead the people of this land to a happier life... and you yourself could have everything you have ever dreamed of — love, possessions, the gratitude of thousands..."

The voice trailed off, waiting for her to reply.

Tenuli did not know what to make of this strange offer. She felt instinctively that the Prince was deceitful, yet her rational mind had to agree with his assessment of her as a good organizer — she *had* handled the domestic matters of the castle well during her short time there. And maybe she *could* control the Prince and force him to help her improve conditions in the Shadowland...

No, no! her inner voice shouted. Do not believe him! It is a trick!

She wrestled with these conflicting pulls within her as the noise of the rainstorm continued to rise. Rivulets of water were running now over the wet ground outside the tent, imitating the sound of a woodland stream.

Bewildered and suddenly very frightened, Tenuli closed her eyes to clear the confusion in her mind, feeling as if her head were splitting apart. 'Help me,' she pleaded in her mind, 'help me!' The noise of the rushing rivulets merged with the drumming of the rain on the tent roof, and it was as if the water's voice spoke to her. Faintly she caught the outline of a white-robed figure standing on alabaster steps before a golden pyramid. "Remember why you are here," said the figure through the watery sound. "Remember why you are here."

Suddenly Tenuli saw how the Prince was deceiving her! He was not the *true* essence of Shadowlanders at all, only the part that was greedy, cruel and selfish! And he was trying to sway her by offering acclaim and wealth! It was the most monstrous temptation to evil that she had ever faced!

With a shudder of disgust she leaped to her feet. "Never!" she shouted, "never in a million years could I cast in my lot with an abomination like you!"

No sooner had she got these words out than a brilliant

113

flash of lightning struck a nearby tree. The instantaneous clap of thunder was deafening. And then, miles away to the east, a strange thing began to happen. The huge mass of stagnant air over the Plains of Mordan started to move in a circle, turning slowly at first then faster and faster. The sparse grass that had never felt even the faintest zephyr of a wind began to bend and rustle as the atmosphere wound itself into a funnel of fury, climbing higher and higher. The cloud layer, pregnant now with magic water from the exploded Well of Tears, roiled and churned into the whirling mass — and then the towering angry funnel began to move over the Plains of Mordan... straight toward the Scarlet Castle.

In the black tent, the Prince had begun to fade away before Tenuli, who was still shaking with revulsion. "Your anger is wasted on me," said the bass voice, sounding now as if it were coming from further away. "But your hatred gives me encouragement, for it means that you still carry a dark seed within you. I shall always try to make that dark seed bring forth its evil fruit, Tenuli, and there may come a time when you will meet me again..."

The voice had grown weak, and the faint image of the Prince was undulating like a flimsy garment in the wind. "Tenuli..." he called in a hoarse whisper, as if summoning what little strength remained. "There was another reason for inviting you into the tent..."

"Which was?"

The answer was hardly audible, as if echoing down a long corridor. "Your friends are desperately looking for you... have not tried to find Korak... by now my trusted servant has escaped..."

The Prince faded out completely, and Tenuli was alone in the tent. The rain was pelting down, and thunder rolled continuously. Fitful flashes of lightning lit the landscape garishly as Tenuli opened the flaps of the black tent and stepped out into the downpour.

Far to the east, the mighty whirlwind struck the Scarlet Castle, howling in fury. The storm first drove great torrential sheets of the magic rain down against the blood-stained stones of its wall — battering them until they were washed clean of the red shame they had carried since the castle's beginning. Then, with a shrieking roar that had never before been heard in the land of shadows, the great wind increased to a horrendous pitch, ripping turrets and battlements apart into flying fragments as it reduced the building to a pile of rubble. And as quickly as it came, it went.

Tenuli peered around her through the falling rain, trying to find her friends. Suddenly a raindrop touched her lips — and her mind burst with the memory of her beloved Moralia! 'The rain!' she thought. 'The rain is acting like the well water!'

"Toth!" she called as she caught sight of the young man riding toward her. "The rain! Have you tasted—"

"Yes!" he shouted back over the din. "It's magnificent! Even the hardened generals are splashing it on their faces and crying like babies!"

"Doesn't it burn them?"

"Seems not. We have a report that the Well of Tears exploded after we left Sandria. Maybe the water mixed with the rainclouds. And maybe its effect was changed."

"Where's Doran?"

"He's with Eluron and the others in the mess-tent. The Knight is talking to a bunch of the soldiers — explaining how things are. Hop on, and we'll ride over."

Tenuli swung up behind her friend, and put her arms about his waist. Smiling, she remembered how she had once reacted in the same situation. Now she felt only the warmth of true affection for this brave young man — affection without any selfish motives attached.

"We never found Korak," said Toth.

"I know," she answered, "you were looking for me instead."

"How do you know?"

"I was talking to the Prince, and he told me."

"What?"

"I found out some interesting things," she said, smiling to herself. "Tell you all about it later."

The Prince had faded away completely from the lower world, because the magic rain had restored to everyone a clear memory of their true home in Moralia and the purpose for sojourning in the land of shadows. That meant there was nobody from whom the Prince could draw his sustenance. Tenuli's temptation had been his final try at retaining a foothold in the Shadowland, but she had seen through the ruse and her refusal had triggered his disintegration. Korak, it seemed, had managed to escape on horseback with a few of his closest henchmen — first to the Northern Outpost, and then across the border into the Desert Lands.

Thanks to Eluron's knowledge of the tunnel entrance at the back of the castle, a special task force of the Knight's followers had been able to rescue the prisoners from the lower dungeons just before the storm destroyed the building. The few guards remaining had been demoralized by the effect of the well water they had tasted in the soup, and offered little resistance. Some were even persuaded to join the Knight's men and flee the castle with them. The others remained, and perished in the the ruins of the evil structure they had chosen to defend.

It was very late when the soldiers and their new-found friends finally bunked in and went to sleep. And while they all slumbered, something wonderful occurred. The seamless blanket of dull cloud that had lain over the lower world ever since anyone could remember began to disperse during the night, due to the magic rainfall. Somehow, the water from the exploded Well of Tears had caused the clouds to rain down all of their moisture, and as a result the grey layer had disappeared.

As dawn approached, a beautiful pink glow suffused itself along the eastern rim of the world, bordering a deep azure canopy spangled with a billion stars. The glow brightened into undulating ribbons of yellow and green, building a painter's pallett of delicate hues. And then, like the first blush of love on a maiden's cheek, like a round golden silent miracle, like the light that shines from everywhere to everywhere in the land beyond the last colour of the last rainbow... the sun of heaven rose glorious and triumphant into the first blue sky.

* * *

Jelander smiled down at the scene. "More than we bargained for, Trillamar?" he said.

"Perhaps our bargains are not the only ones that are struck," mused the other.

And a voice in Jelander's head said, "Perhaps Trillamar is right, my son."

* * * *

And perhaps this is as good a place as any to end the story of Tenuli and the Scarlet Castle.

Dear Reader:

We have called *The Scarlet Castle* the 'First Book of Moralia', thus implying that there will be other volumes in the series. However the author has many other projects that compete for his time, and has indicated that he will tackle a 'Second Book of Moralia' only if reader response to this book is favorable. It would thus help us greatly to know your reaction to *The Scarlet Castle*. We invite you to write to Marcus Books, 195 Randolph Road, Toronto, Canada, M4G 3S6, and give us your views. Please tell us your age, something of your interests, and what you enjoyed most about *The Scarlet Castle*. Would you like to read a 'Second Book of Moralia'? Thank you for helping us in this way.

The Publishers